QUEEN IN LINGERIE

LINGERIE #4

PENELOPE SKY

CONTENTS

Hartwick Publishing

Queen in Lingerie

Copyright © 2018 by Penelope Sky

All rights reserved.

1

CONWAY

MY RAGE LASTED FOR TWO DAYS.

I was pissed about everything. I was pissed she fucked up our relationship by admitting her feelings so publicly. I was angry she accused me of loving her in return. And I was particularly livid about that final comment she made to me—that my parents would be disappointed in me.

She knew exactly how to push my buttons.

In my fury, I banished her from my home. I didn't want her in my bed anymore. I didn't want her presence in the house at all. I wanted to wipe away any evidence she'd ever been there at all.

I wanted her gone.

I wanted her memory forgotten.

I didn't love her, and I warned her not to love me. Now the world thought we were happy together, that I was in love with this woman.

When it was all a lie.

I hadn't gone into my bedroom since she left. I stayed in a guest bedroom, using the clothes Dante picked up for me at the store. Everything I wore was new, and it was a much better alternative to walking inside that horrific room.

I would have asked Dante to clean it up and remove any evidence that she'd been there.

But I couldn't bring myself to do it.

On the third day, my rage finally started to plummet. The exhaustion from not sleeping was getting to me, and the hunger in my stomach was making me weak. I finally had to eat something and sleep. Once I woke up, I was a new man.

And I could think clearly.

Was she okay?

It was the first thought that came to my mind. My men had tried to give her three hundred thousand dollars in cash, but she threw it across the lawn and sped off into the night. She didn't have any money, not even a cent. Unless she sold the car, she had no way of paying for anything.

Fuck, I hoped she sold the car.

I tried to convince myself that kicking her out was the smart thing to do. Our relationship was dead the second she made that confession, and we would never be what we once were. I had to get rid of her and move on with my life.

But I couldn't stop worrying about her.

It was a cruel place out there. Was she alright? Did Knuckles make a move the second she was no longer under my protection?

What the fuck was I thinking when I kicked her out in the middle of the night?

Fuck.

By the fourth day, I couldn't take it anymore. I caved and called her.

But the phone didn't ring. It didn't even go to voice mail.

The number didn't exist.

Fuck. Fuck. Fuck.

Now I couldn't even trace her. What did that mean? Did she ditch the phone so I could never call her again? Or did someone take her and destroy the phone so I couldn't track her down? What if someone had her tied up?

I couldn't breathe.

I called the number again in the hope it was just a mistake.

But it did the exact same thing.

Fuck.

A FEW DAYS LATER, DANTE KNOCKED ON MY OFFICE door. "I'm sorry to bother you, sir—"

"I'm not hungry." Dante had been trying to get me to eat, but I didn't have an appetite. I just kept drinking. I sat at my desk with my hands covering my face, stuck in the mental torture I forced upon myself.

"There's someone here returning the car you loaned to Sapphire. I just thought you might want to know."

My head snapped up and my hands dropped. "Right now?"

"Yes."

I jumped out of my seat and sprinted three flights of stairs until I sped through the entryway and to the outside. The red Ferrari was there, shiny and sleek like it'd been washed. Two men were walking back to a blacked-out car to prepare to leave.

"Wait." I caught up with them before they could get into the car. "Where is she? Who are you?" I got in the man's face, ready to kill him if he'd laid a hand on Muse.

"Who?" he asked. "I'm just dropping off the car."

"Who told you to drop off the car?"

He shrugged. "That's confidential. I'm just paid to do what I'm told."

My heart was slamming against my ribs. I wouldn't be surprised if some of them broke from the force my heart was exerting. "Who do you work for? Who the fuck paid you?"

He raised both hands and stepped back. "Man, I'm just a courier service. When people move or whatever, they ask us to return their shit. The keys were at the office when I got to work, and I was told to drop the car off at this address. That's all I know."

I finally let him go, feeling the relief in my chest. If it was Knuckles or someone else, they wouldn't return my car. They would keep it. Muse obviously wanted me to have it back when she no longer needed it. And if it were Knuckles, he would leave a note.

He would want me to know he had her.

The men drove away.

I stood in the roundabout with my hands on my hips, still terrified by the turn of events. I'd let my anger get to me, and now I found myself in a worse situation than I was in before. I could pretend I didn't give a damn about her, but that wasn't true.

I did care about her.

And I had to know she was okay.

I had to.

2

SAPPHIRE

New York was exactly the same as it was before.

Overcrowded, polluted, and loud. I couldn't see anything in the distance because there was always a building in the way. Direct sunlight was impossible to feel because the skyscrapers cast shadows everywhere.

But it was home.

Andrew lived in a large penthouse with his wife and two sons. At ten thousand square feet, it was a mansion at the top of the building. It wasn't a three-story Italian villa, but it was still a dream house. Decorated fabulously by a professional, it definitely felt like a home for his family. It must have cost him over fifty million dollars to own a piece of real estate like that.

He was nice enough to let me stay there since I had nowhere else to go. He offered to give me money, but I refused to take anything unless it was a paycheck—wages for work I had done.

So in the meantime, I was staying with him.

I had a private bedroom with my own bathroom, and his two sons were hardly ever home because they were both in private school. When they weren't studying, they were participating in their other academic activities. His wife was involved in their education, so she joined her two sons everywhere.

I was home alone most of the time.

My floor-to-ceiling windows gave a wonderful view of the city, but whenever I looked outside, I was always disappointed there were no golden fields to stare at. There were no vineyards or ancient castles. There was no breeze. The windows were sealed in place, so I couldn't even crack them open.

The two places couldn't be more different.

When I arrived in America, my phone stopped working,

so I tossed it in the garbage. Andrew got me a new one, so I carried that with me everywhere I went. I wondered if Conway would ever call me and realize I didn't have that phone anymore.

I'd like to believe he would. But maybe he wouldn't.

I had his car returned to him when I left. I didn't want to leave it on the side of the road for someone to steal. I wanted to make sure when I left I didn't take anything of his with me. The clothes in my bag were all paid for by him, but leaving those behind wouldn't make much of a statement.

I still proved I didn't need him.

A week had come and gone, and I was finally used to the time change. When I went to sleep, Conway woke up. And when he went to sleep, my day was already started. We pretty much lived on different planets at this point.

Now I could move on and forget about him.

Forget about the only man I've ever loved.

My first.

I was still crying over him every night, still living with the deep pain in my chest from his rejection. Who knew confessing my true feelings would drive him away like that? A part of me wished I'd never said anything to begin with.

I'd still be sleeping with him.

I'd still be happy.

But now I had to move on and start over. I had to say goodbye to Vanessa and the rest of the Barsettis.

I had to say goodbye to the love of my life.

ANDREW GAVE ME A WEEK TO GET BACK ON MY FEET before he put me to work. He took me to his studio the following day, a large skyscraper in Manhattan. I used to pass by the building every single day on my way to work, and I never thought I would actually be able to walk inside.

His studio was much bigger than Conway's, covered in lighter tones like white and blue. It was commercialized, reminding me of something I'd seen in a fashion catalogue. Conway surrounded himself in masculine colors, painting the area around him to match his dark mood.

I needed to stop comparing the two designers.

Andrew showed me around the facility, introduced me to the other models, and then escorted me into his office.

"Let's get down to business, shall we?"

I crossed my legs and looked at him over the desk, seeing the city behind him. It was overcast with thick rain clouds, but according to the weather, it wasn't supposed to rain until tomorrow. Fall had arrived in New York far sooner than it arrived in Italy. "Sure."

He was a man in his forties with kindness in his eyes. He brought his hands together on the desk in front of me. He was nothing like Conway. He was transparent, polite, and easy to talk to. He didn't possess the intensity Conway did. Perhaps that was why the designers had such different levels of success.

Conway was a young man at the peak of his sexual exploration. He was bedding all kinds of women, experiencing new things constantly. But Andrew was happily married to the same woman he'd been with for twenty years. He was a father of two boys, making him a family man.

But Conway was right, after all. Marrying me would only destroy his inspiration.

"Alright," Andrew said. "The last offer I extended was three-hundred million. I'm willing to keep that amount, but I have a few terms."

I'd told him Conway and I had gone our separate ways, so I expected him to lower the price since I didn't have any other options. The fact that he didn't made me respect him, made me see him as a nice guy. "What are they?"

"This is a ten-year commitment. You model for me and no one else."

That was more than fair. "Alright."

"The ten-year contract will cover the full amount I've offered. So, for the first year, you would receive thirty million dollars."

That was more than enough. I couldn't even grasp what it would be like to have that kind of money.

"I'll pay that up front, that way you can get properly settled. In the event that you break this contract, you'll have to return everything I've paid you, plus a twenty-percent fee. Your responsibilities include participation in the fashion shows and lots of photographs. You're going to be my biggest model, so expect to see your face plastered everywhere. If all those terms are agreeable to you, we can add our signatures."

He was more than generous, and I could commit to those responsibilities. I wouldn't be able to eat as much anymore, but it was a necessary sacrifice. "That's fair."

"Alright." He grabbed a pen and pushed the contract toward me. "Sign and date here."

I hesitated before I filled it out, missing Conway as I stared at the contract. I used to be his muse, the inspiration for everything he made. But then he turned his back on me, treated me like I'd done something unforgivable simply by loving him. He hurt me so much, and I was grateful I got something out of the ordeal. It wasn't the career I wanted, but it was a career that would pay the bills.

I signed it.

"Great." Andrew added his signature. "Welcome to Lady Lingerie. We're happy to have you, Sapphire."

3

CONWAY

Another week went by.

My waistline was slimmer, and my sleep was even worse.

I didn't get any work done–not because my inspiration was no longer around, but because I was so worried about her.

My muse.

I needed to know if she was alright.

In my heart, I believed she was. But I needed to see it with my own eyes. I needed to hear her tell me she was okay. I knew my pain wasn't from missing her. It was simply from the protectiveness ingrained in my mind.

But her phone never came back online, and none of my guys had seen her in Milan or anywhere else. I was combing the streets looking for her, but I was trying to be discreet about it because if I announced that Muse was missing, Knuckles would see it as a perfect opportunity to snatch her.

If he didn't already have her.

When I got desperate enough, I called Carter.

We met at Club Lingerie in the middle of the day. There was hardly anyone there, so we sat at the bar and ordered round after round. He turned on his stool and stared at me, looking at my full beard with pity. "I want to ask what's wrong, but I already know."

"You do, huh?" I asked before I downed more scotch.

"You ditched her."

No, I did something worse than that.

"What the fuck are you thinking? So what if the woman loves you? You should feel like a king hearing a woman like that pledge her undying love for you—on camera. Even if you don't feel the same way, which I doubt."

I dragged my hand down my face.

"Con, if you want her back, just tell her. She'll give you another chance."

"It's more complicated than that…"

"How?"

I told him the story, up until the point where she had my car returned.

Carter wore a look of pure shock. "You kicked her out of your house? When she doesn't have a dollar on her?"

"I gave her three hundred thousand dollars—but she didn't take it."

"Still. You're a fucking asshole."

I didn't argue with him. "I know."

"And the fact that she didn't take it makes her a class act. Don't you get it, Con? She's never wanted you for your money or your cars. She wants you for you. How many rich men can say that about their women?"

I understood I was lucky. I never doubted that for a second.

"You need to fix this before it's too late."

"I can't."

"Why?"

It hurt to say the words out loud. "I can't find her..."

"You can find anyone."

"I've tried—and failed. That's why I'm here with you. I need your help."

He breathed in his cigar and let the smoke escape through his nostrils. "My help?"

"Yes."

"Your dad would be the best person to turn to."

When Muse said my parents would be disappointed in me, she hit a nerve. It hurt because it was true. "I'm not asking him for help unless I absolutely have to."

"Why?"

"You think I want him to know about all this?" I snapped. "The story won't make sense unless I tell him everything. And he already has a pretty low opinion of me right now, and I'm ready to dig my own grave."

"Alright." Carter finally let it go. "We should check the airlines first. She may have been able to buy a ticket in cash or on someone else's card, but she can't lie on the manifest. She's from New York, right?"

"Yeah, but I don't think she would go there. She really loves Italy."

"But she doesn't have any money, so what else would she do?" he asked. "I can have my guys check the listings. What's her last name?"

I drank the rest of my glass.

He pulled out his phone to take the note. "Con?"

I closed my eyes before I said it. "I don't know…"

Carter's look was even more incredulous. "You're shitting me."

"When we first met, she wouldn't tell me her last name. She was running from Knuckles and the Feds."

"And you didn't think to ask her later? In all the months you were fucking her?"

I wanted to slam the glass over his head. "I don't know her last name, alright? Let it go."

"Con, this is going to make it a million times harder."

"Just check the damn flights and see if there's anyone named Sapphire on there." I was going on little sleep and nearly no food, so my patience was at an all-time low. The stress was eating me alive.

"Alright, I'll try," he said. "But passengers are organized by last name. So we may not find anything."

"We'll figure out what to do then." I waved the bartender over and demanded a refill. When my glass was full, I took another drink.

Carter stared at me for a while.

I felt his gaze on my profile. "Whatever you have to say, I don't want to listen to it."

"Yeah, you're probably right. But I'm going to say it anyway."

I sighed.

"Sapphire called me the night she left."

I slowly turned to him, caught off guard. "Why?"

"She wanted to know why you were being so cold to her...so I told her. In the beginning, she was confused.

She didn't believe me because she was so confident that you loved her too."

She'd told me the same thing.

"And then she started crying. She hid it pretty well...but I could hear it."

As if someone punched me in the stomach, I felt winded.

"You broke this woman's heart, man. And that would be fine if you didn't love her...but it's obvious you do. Is that really such a bad thing?"

"I told her I didn't want marriage and shit..."

"Doesn't change the fact that you love her. She didn't ask you to marry her. All she said was she loved you."

"But you know where it would lead..."

"And maybe if you gave it some time, you might have actually liked the idea. But you flipped out and fucked it up before you even gave it a chance."

"Carter, when have we ever talked about this shit?" I snapped. "Now you're talking about love like you know things...when you don't know anything."

"You're right," he said calmly. "I don't know a lot of things. But I know when a man loves a woman, and you love her. I just hope by the time we find her that she still loves you...or loves you enough to forgive you for what you did."

4

SAPPHIRE

WITH MY FIRST PAYCHECK, I BOUGHT A CONDO.

I paid for it in cash, that way I would never have to worry if I could afford it or not. It wasn't super fancy like Andrew's place, but it was a nice unit with twenty-five hundred square feet. It had a great view of the park, it was close to the gym, and it was walking distance to the Lady Lingerie building.

I couldn't ask for anything better.

Independence was invigorating. I didn't have to rely on anyone for anything, and I missed that feeling. It had been difficult to become dependent on Conway, but once I did, it felt nice. But then he flipped on me and kicked me out on my ass.

And I realized how weak I was.

Now I wasn't weak anymore. I had food on the table, property, and money in the bank.

It wasn't a villa in Italy, and living alone was extremely lonely. I wore Conway's t-shirts every night because I needed them like a security blanket.

A part of me hoped he would come for me, that he would realize he couldn't live without me.

That he loved me.

It hurt so much to say those words and not have him say it back. It hurt to see how angry my love made him. It turned a perfect man into a raging monster. The idea of being happy and in love with a woman was really that repulsive to him.

It killed me.

I STOOD IN THE HEELS ANDREW GAVE ME, THE PUMPS silver and sparkling. They were painful like any other shoes I wore, but I had to tough it out. I was getting paid enough for the discomfort.

I dropped my robe and stood in the silver lingerie Andrew had me try on.

He sat in the red armchair, looking at me like he wasn't impressed.

I straightened my shoulders even more, perfecting my posture the way Conway taught me.

But Andrew didn't react. "What do you think?"

"About what?" I asked.

"About this bodysuit. What would make it better?"

I looked at my reflection in the mirror. The bodysuit was simple, skintight with a bow at the top. It didn't have a lot of texture to it, and it seemed overly boring. "I have no idea...it looks nice to me."

"What would Conway do?"

The question was immediately unwelcome. It made me think it was a cut into my brain, an investigation into what I knew about Conway. I'd seen him design his pieces regularly, but I had no idea what happened in his mind. And even if I did, I would never stoop that low. Even though he turned out to be an asshole who broke my heart, he still treated me right. I had to honor that. "I have no idea. His pieces are pretty simple too."

"You really have no recommendations?" he asked.

"I just model the lingerie, Andrew. Conway didn't include me in the design process."

"But he used you as inspiration, yes?"

"Yes," I said. "But again, I don't know how."

Andrew turned back to his sketchbook and made a few marks. He looked up at me from time to time. "This piece needs a lot more work. But when I'm done, I'd like to photograph you for an ad spread in *Vogue*. Would that be alright?"

I wasn't paid to say no. "Of course."

"Great. Give me a few more days, and I'll get back to you."

———

I stared at my phone when I was home.

I kept expecting Conway's number to appear on the screen.

Was he thinking about me? Did he ever think about me?

Had he already fucked someone else by now?

I couldn't let my thoughts go there—not if I didn't want to drown in misery.

I allowed myself a glass of wine after my meager dinner of a piece of salmon and veggies. Now I was expected to remain a certain size, so my favorite meals were no longer available. With Conway, he never cared about my waistline. He didn't treat me differently at my heaviest or my thinnest.

I sat on the hardwood floor in front of the floor-to-ceiling window. My wineglass was beside me, and I wore Conway's black t-shirt. It was loose on my arms and my waist, and it stretched all the way down to my knees.

I stared at the city lights that surrounded the park. It was a beautiful view, but it didn't compare to the one I saw on that hilltop with Conway. Verona looked beautiful under the sunlight, absolutely stunning.

He showed me so many beautiful things.

I wondered what his life was like now. Did he throw away all my belongings? Was he sleeping in the bed we shared together? It'd been two weeks since the last time we'd made love. Did he miss being between my legs? Did he miss it as much as I did?

Did he have any regrets about the way we left things?

All I had to do was call him to find out.

But what if he didn't have any regrets? What if he hadn't thought about me once since I left? What if he was annoyed that I called him?

How would I ever recover from that?

The risk was too great, so I chickened out.

WHEN ANDREW FINISHED DESIGNING THE PIECE, I wore it for the photoshoot.

It was my first one.

I had no experience at all, so I tried to pretend I was on the runway. I focused on my posture and my presence. I didn't smile because Conway told me I should never smile when I was on camera.

He told me to be sexy...even though that advice wasn't necessarily helpful.

I lay back on a bed, the purple comforter and pillow contrasting against the silver lingerie I wore. The photographer moved my hair in different ways, making sure the lighting hit me just right.

This was different from the runway because this was a single moment in time that was being captured. It would be in magazines all over the world, and there was no doubt Andrew would have it on billboards too.

I was about to be in the spotlight again.

I just wondered how long it would take Conway to notice.

And if he did notice...would he care?

5

CONWAY

AFTER THREE WEEKS, I COULDN'T AVOID IT ANYMORE.

I had to go back into my bedroom.

I hadn't stepped inside since Muse had vacated the premises. She could have looted some of my stuff for all I knew.

Even though she never would.

I held my breath as I walked inside, expecting complete destruction. She had been in such a hurry, she might have knocked things over as she stormed out. She was pissed, so she might have shattered the TV and tipped the table over.

But the sitting room was exactly the same.

I moved across the room to the bedroom. Once I stepped over the threshold, I saw the chaos. The closet doors were still open, and a lot of her dresses had fallen off their hangers and onto the floor. Her drawer was pulled open, and most of her panties were gone.

I stepped farther into the room, seeing the piles on the bed that she left behind. She probably meant to take them with her but she didn't have room in her bag. It was a shame, because I bought her the most gorgeous clothes money could buy.

But she had to leave them behind because I threw her out.

I noticed the champagne dress with the diamonds along the straps. It was beautiful, and I found it odd that it was sitting on the ground directly underneath my dresser. When my eyes moved up, I noticed my drawer was still slightly open. It was where I kept my t-shirts, a drawer that Muse used just as much as I did.

I opened it and looked inside.

Half of my shirts were missing.

She took them.

Despite what I did, she still wanted a piece of me. And

she left one of her favorite dresses behind to make sure she had room for them.

This was exactly why I hadn't wanted to come in here.

Because I knew I would feel like this.

Like shit.

I sat at the foot of the bed and rested my elbows on my knees. My hands cupped my skull, and I breathed through the ferocity, breathed through my regret. The last six months of our relationship had been erased in a single night.

Because of me.

My phone vibrated in my pocket, and I pulled it out to see Carter's name on the screen.

I answered it. "Tell me some good news."

"Actually, I do have some good news. But I have some pretty shitty news too."

I closed my eyes and rubbed my skull. "I want the bad news first...but only if that means she's alright. If she's not alright, just don't say anything. I can't bear it..." I'd never been this scared to face the truth. But I'd never cared about something so much that it made me this vulnerable.

"Alright...I haven't found her. But I know she's okay."

I released the breath I was holding. "Thank fucking god. What's the bad news?" Now I could handle anything he said.

He sighed into the phone. "You aren't going to like it..."

"Just tell me, Carter."

"Well...she's modeling for Andrew Lexington now."

I heard the words loud and clear, but my brain didn't work as quickly as my ears. "How...how do you know this?"

"Because I found a picture of a photoshoot she did for him."

"You're sure it's her?"

"There's no mistake, man. And if I were you...I wouldn't look at it."

A jolt of jealousy and possessiveness rocked through me, making my jaw clench so hard my teeth almost shattered. This was the one time I would take his advice.

"That means she must be in New York. But you didn't see her on any of the flights."

"Yeah, I'm not sure how that happened. Must be because of her last name."

It'd only been three weeks since she left, and she already managed to make a deal with one of my competitors. How did he find her that quickly? Or did she go to him?

"Are you going to call him?"

That was a dead end. "He tried to get a hold of her a few months ago, but I wouldn't put him through. If I call, he won't help me."

"Too bad you burned that bridge..."

I had been too possessive of her at the time. And I should have stayed possessive of her. "She must be in New York. I know where his office is, so I should be able to wait outside until she walks in."

"You're just going to ambush her?" he asked.

"You got a better idea, asshole?" I countered.

"Hey, I'm trying to help you here, asshole," he snapped. "I say you have someone tail her and find out where she lives. Show up there. That way you have some privacy to talk. Talking outside Lady Lingerie isn't going to get you far."

"Yeah, you're probably right."

"When are you heading out, then?"

It was already one in the morning, but I knew I wouldn't be able to sleep tonight anyway. "Right now."

"You want me to come with you?"

I knew he would tag along to be supportive, but he had other things to worry about. "No. I'll handle this alone."

"Alright. Good luck, man."

"Thanks...for all your help." No matter how stupid I was, I knew I could always turn to Carter to help me out.

"No problem. But Conway, if you're lucky enough to get her to listen to you, don't fuck it up again. You may not get another chance."

———

LAST TIME I WAS IN NEW YORK, MUSE WAS MY DATE to my biggest fashion show. Everyone looked at how beautiful she was, how stunning she was on my arm. She was my woman at the time, the woman I took back to my hotel and made love to.

She was the only woman I ever made love to.

Now I was back, but this time, she wasn't with me.

It was evening when I arrived, so I got some rest and showered the next morning. My PI was ready to follow her once she made her move, and he got me the details I wanted to know by the end of the day.

She lived across the street from Central Park, in a building that was for homeowners only.

Which meant she bought some real estate.

And that also meant Andrew was paying her well.

But he'd better only be paying her for her work in front of the camera—and nothing else.

After she finished her day of work, she went to the gym down the street. So I waited outside her condo door for her, waiting for the time to trickle by until she returned. I wasn't even sure what I was going to say to her when I saw her.

I'm sorry?

Could I really apologize after being the biggest dick on the planet? Would an apology mean something to this woman who was kicked out on her ass? If I apologized a hundred times, would it ever erase my stupid decision?

She shouldn't forgive me.

She shouldn't have loved me in the first place.

An hour later, her footsteps sounded around the corner. I knew it was her before she was visible because I recognized her footfalls. After living with her for months, I knew all the small details about her, even the way her small feet hit the hardwood as she moved. I knew the quiet sighs she would make when she was about to fall asleep. I knew the way she always touched her hair when she looked in the mirror, slightly self-conscious about her appearance.

She rounded the corner in black leggings and a tight t-shirt. Her long hair was pulled back into a ponytail, and her face was slightly flushed from the workout she'd just had. She didn't wear any makeup, and that highlighted her perfect complexion. Her eyes were focused on her hands as she moved her keys around until she found the right one.

She didn't notice me until she almost bumped into me.

The keys fell to the floor, making a loud rattle once metal hit wood.

She inhaled a quick breath in surprise, her hand still extended where her keys should be. Based on her large eyes and the pure shock on her face, I was the last thing she expected to see when she rounded the corner.

My eyes took in her face, seeing the perfect skin without any hint of a bruise. She wore expensive workout clothes, and her hair was properly taken care of. She looked healthy and glowing, no sign of trauma or abuse.

I was so fucking relieved.

She held my gaze, the surprise slowly fading away and annoyance taking over. Now she was angry with me, livid after the way we left things.

As she should be.

"What do you want, Conway?" Cold, malicious, and angry, she didn't hold back.

I blocked the door so she couldn't dart inside and slam it in my face. "Can I come in?"

She bent down and picked up her keys, her eyebrows furrowed in displeasure. "I don't want my neighbors to hate me, so that's probably a good idea." She unlocked the door then stepped inside.

I could have let myself into her apartment and waited for her to return, but I didn't want to piss her off the second she saw me.

She was already pissed off enough.

I stepped inside her place and saw the elegant decor she had. It reminded me of my house in Italy, and I wondered if she did that on purpose. There was a nice living room, a full kitchen, and a dining room. The hallway turned to the left, and I suspected it led to several different bedrooms.

"You have a nice place." She'd done very well for herself in only three weeks. I shouldn't have underestimated her.

"Thanks." She set her bag down and dropped her keys into the bowl. She turned around and faced me, her arms crossed over her chest. She didn't look at me with the affectionate gaze she used to have. She didn't rake her eyes over my body with lust. Now she stared at me like I was nothing but a nuisance. "What do you want, Conway?"

I slid my hands into the pockets of my jeans and admired her trim body. She was beautiful, perfect like she was when she'd left my home. With her pretty eyes glued to my face, I didn't know where to start. "I've been trying to call you for a while."

Her arms tightened, and her gaze remained as cold as ever. "It didn't work here, so I got rid of it."

I gave a slight nod. "I was really worried about you...I searched everywhere for you."

"If you were that worried, maybe you shouldn't have thrown me out in the middle of the night." She didn't raise her voice, but her clipped tone showed her heavy resentment.

I didn't have a comeback to that because she was totally right. My temper peaked, and I lost control of my faculties. "You're right. I shouldn't have done that. I wish I could take it back."

"You can't, Conway. There are some things you can't take back...that's one of them."

I closed my eyes for a moment, her anger burning me all the way down to the bone. I didn't have a rebuttal because there was nothing that could justify my behavior. It didn't matter how pissed I had been. "I want you to know I'm sorry...even if that means nothing to you. I haven't slept much because I've been so terrified that something happened to you. I had all my guys combing the streets for you. My life has been flipped upside down. The rare times that I could sleep, I had nightmares that Knuckles got you. If you think I've just returned to my former life, I haven't. I've done nothing but suffer this entire time."

Her eyes shifted to the floor.

"I asked Carter to help me find you. He saw your photo in *Vogue*. That's how I tracked you down here."

She still didn't give a reaction.

I glanced around the apartment again. "Andrew is treating you well?"

"Yes," she said coldly. "He hasn't made me his prisoner."

I deserved that.

"He offered me three hundred million for a ten-year contract."

Even I had to react to a sum like that. My eyes dilated and my pulse quickened.

"So I'll pay you back for saving me from Knuckles. I don't want to owe you anything."

"You don't."

"Yes, I do."

I'd pay that money again in a heartbeat to keep her safe. "I won't take it, so don't bother. We're square."

She shifted her weight to one leg, still closed off from me.

"I like your place."

"Thanks..."

Now our conversation came to a halt. It was tense and awkward, and there wasn't much to say. This woman was such an important part of my life, and now she was a stranger. She used to share my bed with me every single night. Now my big bed felt even bigger than before.

She lowered her arms to her sides and sighed. "Now that you know I'm alright, you should go. We both have important lives to return to."

I'd said what I wanted to say, and now I had no business being there. But I didn't want to move. I wanted to stare at her face forever. I didn't want to return to my mansion in Italy, not when I was the only one to enjoy it.

She looked at me, her disappointment obvious. "Go."

Instead of walking to the door, I walked up to her. I stopped when our faces were close together. When she didn't take a step back, I knew there was something still between us. "I'm miserable without you."

She took a deep breath and held it, her beautiful eyes slightly glossy.

"I hate what I did. I don't want you to think you don't mean anything to me...because that's not true. These past three weeks have been some of the worst of my life, if not the worst." My hands moved to her hips, and when she didn't resist me, I felt a surge of hope in my chest. "I lost my temper, and I shouldn't have treated you that way. It was stupid...really fucking stupid." I pressed my forehead against hers.

She let me touch her. She rested her arms on mine, her breathing quickened.

I thought I would forget about her the second she was off my property, but I'd thought about her more when she was gone than when she was around. My chest felt hollow because all my joy had been stripped away. I felt lost, like I would never find happiness ever again. Now that she was in my arms again, I felt better. "Please forgive me, Muse."

She closed her eyes when I said her nickname, the name I always should have been calling her. There was no reason the name Sapphire should have escaped my mouth. It didn't even sound right on my tongue. I felt repulsive saying it out loud.

"Conway...I don't care about giving you my forgiveness."

My hand slid into her hair, and I cupped her cheek, my thumb brushing across the soft skin. I missed touching her this way, missed feeling her warmth. I hadn't gotten laid in almost a month, and while I missed the sex, I missed this a lot more—the intimacy. She was the only woman I showed any vulnerability with. She was the only woman who had earned my kiss.

"All I want is for you to tell me you love me." Her eyes lifted up to meet my gaze. "To forget that horrific night and just start over. I don't want to forgive you because I'd rather forget." She held my gaze as she waited for me to say the words, for me to echo the love that was in her heart.

My thumb stopped brushing against her cheek, and I held my breath as I stared at her. She had every part of me, all of my thoughts, my emotions, and my body. I didn't want to share my bed with anyone else. But I didn't want to commit to a life I'd told her I didn't want. "I told you I would never marry you."

"Did I ask you to marry me?" she whispered. "I just want to love you—and have you love me in return. The future is blurry and uncertain, but that's how it's supposed to be. Anything can happen. The door is always open to potential—and you should never close it. Closing off possibilities is only a disservice to yourself."

My hand slowly slid down to her neck, her wisdom striking me hard.

"Do you really not love me, Conway? Or do you just not want to?"

My hand moved to her shoulder then slid down her arm. The backs of my forefingers brushed against her soft skin. The farther I moved, the colder I felt. When my hand pulled away entirely, it was like stepping into the Arctic. "I want exactly what we had before. I want to give you all of me, and I want to take all of you. I want us to live together in that beautiful mansion and make beautiful lingerie together. I want it to stay that way... until it's run its course. I don't know where I'll be in five or ten years. And whether I tell you I love you or not, it doesn't make a difference. Even if I did say it, that doesn't mean I won't leave you. Because, one day, I will. And I would never mislead you about my intentions."

Her eyes stayed the same, but the moisture on the surface slightly deepened. She didn't frown or take a deep breath. As a prideful woman, she held her stance of power. "I'm not ashamed to tell you that I love you, that I want to spend the rest of my life with you. I don't care about your yacht in Greece or the beautiful clothes you buy me. I want to sleep every night with you beside me, to listen to your deep breathing while you dream. I want to be pregnant with your son or daughter, to become your wife in a pretty white dress. I want to be your inspiration always, no matter how much my body changes or how I age. I want us to be together forever, to be buried underneath the same tombstone. I can say all of that without shame, even as you look at me with rejection, because it's real. And I can't settle for some of you. I can't love you with my whole heart if you won't do the same. As much as I love you, I know I deserve better." She released a quiet sigh, her eyes welling up further. "I'll never forget our time together. You changed my life in so many good ways. I'll never forget the way the Italian sun feels against my skin, the way you sat across from me on the terrace when we had breakfast every morning. I'll never forget our nights together, how you took me when I was innocent and made me into a woman. I have a lot of happy memories...but that's all you'll ever be. A memory. One day, I'll meet someone else and fall in love again. I'll get married and have children, and there will always be a slight pain because you aren't the man I'm married to. But in time, those memories will fade. And maybe one day...I'll forget them altogether." When she blinked, two tears streaked down her cheeks.

It killed me to see them.

She rose on her tiptoes and cupped my face before she placed a kiss on my mouth. It was slow and soft, slightly salty from her tears. She breathed with me, feeling my upper lip between hers. She slowly pulled away, her eyes wet and red. "Goodbye, Conway."

MUSE DIDN'T NEED ME.

She was rich and safe, living in a great apartment in a safe building.

From what I heard, Andrew was happily married and a well-known family man. When he wasn't working, he was seen with his two sons at baseball practice and academic decathlon. But even the happiest man could succumb to temptation when a woman like Muse was around.

Walking out of her apartment was one of the hardest things I've ever had to do. I wanted to keep kissing her and guide her into the bedroom so I could make love to her one last time, but that would only make it harder.

On both of us.

So I took my plane back to Italy.

I left her behind.

I slept on the plane, which was the longest amount of time I'd slept since she left.

Now that I knew she was okay, saw it with my own eyes, I could finally relax.

I returned to Verona and walked into the home I bought almost ten years ago. When I bought it, I knew it was big for just a single man. But the previous owner needed to sell the house quickly because he'd lost his company. He gave me an unbelievable deal, so I moved in to the enormous mansion.

Dante greeted me when I walked inside. "Hello, sir. How was your trip?"

I wasn't in the mood for small talk. "Fine. I'm not hungry right now. I'll take dinner in a few hours."

"Of course." He walked with me to the stairs. "Sir?"

"Yes, Dante?"

"I hate to ask but...will Miss Sapphire be returning?"

I stopped at the bottom stair and gripped the rail of the staircase. The question annoyed me, but I couldn't blame him for wondering. "No."

Dante gave a slight nod, but there was no hiding the disappointment in his eyes. "Would you like me to remove all of her things from your bedroom?"

I didn't want to throw anything away, but I didn't want to see her clothes every time I opened my closet. I didn't want to see her panties in my dresser. I didn't want to see her old perfume in the bathroom. Everything would remind me of her, and I didn't want to be reminded of the woman who changed my life. "Yes...but don't throw it away." I didn't want to keep her things because I hoped she would come back one day. I just couldn't bear seeing her stuff thrown in the garbage.

"Of course." He gave another nod and turned away.

"Dante?"

He turned back around.

"I didn't realize you were so fond of her." I'd never seen them interact, and he was put off when she tried to help herself in the kitchen. After that, they didn't interact very often.

"I'm not," he said. "I just know she made you happy."

TIME MOVED SO SLOWLY.

I stopped working out and spent my time in my room.

It rained one day, and it was the first rain of the season. It poured on the rooftop, and the sound of the rain was loud when the Tuscan-style windows were open. I wished she could have seen it. All she'd ever known was the constant sunshine. Something about the rainfall was peaceful, even when you were forced to stay inside.

I found myself thinking about her a lot, wondering what she was doing. Did she like modeling for Andrew? Were the other women treating her right? Was she getting used to New York again? Or did she still miss Italy?

I went to work in Milan later that week, and I didn't feel any motivation when I walked through the doors. The only reason I was there was because I didn't know what else to do with my time.

I sat in the studio and stared at my sketchbook, no idea what to draw. All I could think about was the last time I saw Muse. The tears streaked down her face, and her eyes were swollen and puffy.

It didn't turn me on like the other times. It broke my heart.

I didn't even know I had a heart until then.

I was tempted to Google her, to see the multitude of images she appeared in. Not only did I want to see her face, but I wanted to see her body. I missed looking at her long legs, at her narrow waist. I wanted to drag my tongue everywhere, to taste her one more time. It'd been a month since she left my house, and it was the longest time I'd gone without getting laid since I hit puberty.

I hadn't even jerked off.

Too depressed.

But now, the arousal was building up inside me. Instead of going out and catching tail, I wanted to be with Muse. I wanted that slow but good sex. I wanted to be skin-to-skin with the woman who'd only had me. I didn't want to wear a condom and fuck a woman I wouldn't remember.

I stared blankly at my sketchbook.

My phone rang, and Carter's name appeared on the screen. I almost didn't answer it, but I knew I couldn't avoid him forever. "What's up?"

"What's up?" he asked incredulously. "I've never heard you say that before."

"First time for everything, right?"

He sighed. "You sound miserable, so I assume you decided to be an idiot."

"Not an idiot. It just didn't work out."

"So, what? It's over."

Losing her was difficult, but I didn't see any other way around it. "Yes."

"And now what?"

"I move on."

"To what, exactly? You aren't going to find another woman like that."

"Maybe. Maybe not."

He sighed again. "Con—"

"Let it go. It's done."

Carter turned quiet. "Fine. Are you going to tell the family soon? How long do I have to keep up the charade?"

I didn't want to tell my family Muse was gone. They might respect my privacy and not ask a lot of questions, but Vanessa would be pissed. "I'm not sure. Not long. Vanessa will figure it out soon enough."

"Alright. Let me know when she does."

"Okay."

"So, is Sapphire happy? How is she?"

I was surprised Carter asked about her. He didn't spend much time with her when I was seeing her, but he obviously had a fondness for her. "She bought a pretty nice place, for three million dollars. It's in a safe area. She likes working for Andrew. She's obviously upset about us…but she's doing really well."

"Good for her. She stands on her own two feet…I admire that."

I did too.

"I think you should think about it a little harder, Con. If you wait too long…that's it."

I'd said my goodbyes. It was time to move on. "Let it go, Carter."

"Fine…I'm officially letting it go."

———

I FELT LIKE A DISGUSTING PERV.

I opened my laptop in bed and found her pictures everywhere. Andrew was using her for a lot of publicity, taking pride in the fact that he had the most beautiful woman in the world working for him.

And Barsetti Lingerie lost her.

His pieces were mediocre, but Muse picked up the slack. She made everything look gorgeous, her long figure so curvy and beautiful. The bras pushed her tits together, and she lay on the bed, like she was waiting for me to move between her legs.

I looked at everything, feeling my dick get so hard it actually hurt.

I hadn't jerked off in a long time, but I was desperate. If I picked up a woman, I would just picture myself with Muse anyway. So I squirted the lotion into my hand and started to jerk myself while staring at her picture.

It was nothing compared to the real thing.

But it was the best I could do.

6

SAPPHIRE

The next two weeks were excruciating.

It was like having all of my ribs broken after a horse kicked me.

I couldn't breathe. I couldn't sleep. I couldn't eat.

Conway left—and it was really over.

He didn't want forever—or anything close to it. He didn't want to love me. He just wanted our passionate relationship to run its course until he got bored. Then he would replace me with someone else. Marriage and kids were completely taken off the table.

He couldn't stand just the possibility.

I supposed this was entirely my fault.

I was stupid for falling in love with him. I should have listened to his warning. Even though I still suspected he loved me, that didn't mean anything. His feelings were irrelevant because he wouldn't act on them.

He was probably fucking someone else by now.

Lots of women.

And I was putting my heart back together.

This depression helped me drop the extra five pounds Andrew wanted me to lose. Not eating really fixed the problem. I still worked out every day, so that made the fat fly off my waistline and disappear from my thighs.

I was getting used to New York, but in my heart, I knew it wasn't home.

Italy was home now.

Conway was my home.

But I had to move forward and start over. I had to be positive and focus on all the things I did have. I was wealthy, had a great job, and there wasn't a psychopath trying to hunt me down anymore. Conway gave me my freedom, so letting him break my heart wasn't completely in vain.

I would move on, and hopefully, I would find another guy to sweep me off my feet.

But it was hard to imagine being with another guy… sleeping with another guy.

Conway was the only guy I'd ever been with.

I would hate all the women who came after me, especially since they didn't care about him for the man he was. They just saw his Ferrari, his wallet, and the big-ass house he slept in every night. They knew nothing about his character, his love for his family, or his generosity.

I was the only woman who truly knew him.

After being at the studio all day, I went home and changed into my workout clothes before I went to the gym. Sometimes people recognized me, judging by the way they stared at me, but thankfully, no one ever asked me for an autograph.

I usually did an hour on the treadmill before I moved to the weights. Andrew assigned me a workout routine, and that made me miss Conway—for other reasons. Conway never asked me to work out. He didn't tell me what to eat either. Whether I was fifteen pounds heavier or not, he wanted me the same.

But Andrew didn't want me for his personal use. He just wanted me to be as thin as possible for the camera.

I missed food. And I missed sitting on my ass all day. I never considered working with the horses to be work because I enjoyed it so much. But going to the gym religiously felt like a chore. There was loud music, bright lights, and lots of people around.

Now I preferred the quiet, open spaces.

I did five squats with the twenty-pound barbell before I returned it to the ground. I wasn't as strong as I used to be. Working in the stables all day had given my legs perfect muscle tone. But it'd been a month since I stopped doing that, and it was taking some time to pick up the strength again.

I wiped my forehead with the back of my forearm and then stood with my hands on my hips. When I looked at my reflection in the mirror, I saw a tall man with dark brown hair walk up to my side. He held two free weights, both heavier than the single barbell I was using.

He started to do biceps curls, a charming smile on his face. His eyes were on me in the mirror. Under his gray shorts, the muscles of his toned legs were visible. His t-shirt hugged his powerful body, showing the outline of his strong arms. But no amount of working out could make his face handsome. That was all natural. "I've been trying to find an excuse to talk to you all week, but I haven't been able to come up with anything original or smart. A woman like you must get hit on all the time, so I tried to think of something witty...but that didn't happen either." He set his weights on the ground and turned to me, his hand extended. "So I'm just going to introduce myself. I'm Nox."

I wasn't looking for a date right now, but he seemed like a nice guy, and I didn't want to be rude. If he wasn't just feeding me a line, then it would be cold to shut him down right off the bat. "Sapphire."

He shook my hand, his blue eyes pretty in contrast to his masculine face. "I thought I recognized you. You're that model."

"Guilty." Without makeup and special clothes, I probably looked like a whole different person. I was surprised he recognized me, even when he knew my name. "It's nice to meet you, Nox. I hope when you've been watching me all week you haven't been laughing at my workouts."

"Never," he said with a chuckle. "You've got great form."

"Thanks to all those YouTube videos I watched."

He smiled. "That's what YouTube is for." He tapped his foot against my barbell. "You're lifting good weight. For someone at your size, that's perfect."

"You seem to know stuff about working out." Since he was all muscle and no fat, I guess that wasn't surprising.

"A thing or two," he said. "I opened this gym five years ago. Fitness is my passion."

"This is your gym?" I asked in surprise.

"Yep. But if you have any complaints, that's for the manager," he said with a laugh.

"No, of course not," I said. "I like it here. There's plenty of space. It's nice."

"Thanks," he said. "This introduction went pretty well. For a supermodel, you're pretty easy to talk to."

Now I laughed. "So not a supermodel."

"So, how about we have dinner tonight?" he asked. "You like sushi?"

I loved sushi. I hadn't had it since I left New York—the first time. It would be nice to get out of my apartment and socialize with someone who wasn't a model or a photographer. And it would be nice to think about someone else besides Conway. But it was way too soon. I was hopelessly hung up on Conway...and I would stay that way for a long time. "You're very charming, Nox. But I'm not dating right now..." My lips fell into a frown. I felt the comfortable air between us slip away when I hit the brakes on our casual conversation.

Nox didn't seem discouraged. "Well, you're still looking for friends, right?"

"You can never have too many friends."

"So how about we just hang out? Two friends getting sushi."

I wanted to say yes, but I couldn't. "I don't want to waste your time."

"I don't think making a new friend is wasting time. How about that place on Fifty-Seventh and Broadway? I'll see you tonight at seven."

If I didn't go out tonight, I would just sit in my apartment all alone. I would watch TV and stop myself from digging into a pint of ice cream. And then I would think about Conway...wondering if he'd just woken up and gotten his day started. The idea was so depressing that I would do anything to avoid that fate.

Avoid picturing him walking up next to someone else.

"Alright," I said. "I'll see you then."

WE EACH ORDERED A SUSHI ROLL AND SHARED THE two varieties. With our chopsticks in hand in the small restaurant, we ate our dinner and enjoyed our sake.

"My dads left me everything they had in their trust, so when it was handed over to me, I decided to invest in something. So I bought three gyms in Manhattan. I have their place near Park Avenue. I could have sold that too, but I decided to keep it. Living there makes me sad sometimes, but it also makes me feel closer to them."

"I'm sorry about the accident...that's terrible."

"It's alright," he said. "It's been a few years now." He placed another piece of sushi into his mouth. "Do you have family in the city?" He didn't ask about my romantic situation and kept our meeting friendly. We talked about work, school, and family. Even though he was just a stranger, he started to feel like a friend by the time we finished dinner.

"No. My brother passed away almost a year ago. My parents have been gone for a while. I'm all that's left..." I tried to dissipate the sadness by drinking my sake and avoiding the sadness in his gaze.

Even when he wore a pitiful gaze, he was still hot. "Looks like we're in the same boat. I don't have any siblings. I never knew my grandparents because they never approved of my father being gay. And my other grandparents both died young. So...I'm all that's left."

"I guess it makes me feel better knowing I'm not the only one."

"And when you have your own family, you'll never feel that way again."

I'd always wanted children, but I pictured having them with Conway. I pictured them having Barsetti looks and strength. With olive skin and beautiful eyes, whether they were boys or girls, it didn't matter. They would be gorgeous.

When I realized I was thinking about Conway, for the tenth time during dinner, I forced myself to stop.

"So, I'm just asking as a friend...what's your romantic situation?" He held his chopsticks in his fingers but didn't take another bite. His blue eyes were on me, watching every move I made. He had the same intensity as Conway, looking at me like I was all that mattered.

I decided to be honest—and blunt. "I'm madly in love with a man...but he doesn't feel the same way." It hurt just as much to say it out loud as it did to say it in my head. But I felt good telling Nox the truth. I didn't want him to waste his time. Most men would be turned off by that confession, and they had every right to be.

But Nox didn't blink. "So, he's a douchebag."

I chuckled because I hadn't expected him to say that. "No...he's a good man. He just doesn't want the same things I want."

"And what do you want?"

I didn't just want marriage, kids, and a happily ever after. "Forever."

His eyes softened. "And this douchebag doesn't want to

spend forever with a sweet and gorgeous model? He really thinks there's something better out there?"

"Don't call him that," I said quietly. I was loyal to Conway, even now. I couldn't stand to hear anyone talk badly about him. He might have broken my heart, but he was a good man. "He's a lingerie designer, so he always has beautiful women who want him."

"Ooh..." He nodded his head slowly. "Conway Barsetti. I think I remember seeing something on TV about you guys. Forgot about it until now."

"Yeah..."

"I don't think it matters how successful or rich he is. You're still out of his league—and that's my professional opinion."

I smiled. "That's a sweet thing to say."

"And thanks for being honest with me. That's really cool of you."

"Like I said, I don't want you to waste your time."

"Waste my time?" he asked. "I'm a patient guy. I don't mind being on the waitlist for a while."

"Waitlist?" I asked.

"Yeah. Eventually, you're going to be ready to start dating. And I'd rather make sure I'm the first name you think of instead of moving on with my life. We can be friends in the meantime. So, basically, I'm wait-listed. Once this guy is out of your head, I'll be the first in line."

"That's really sweet. But honestly, you're out of my league."

He chuckled like I made a joke.

"I'm serious. You could find some other super awesome woman."

He shook his head. "I've been in the dating game for a while now. There's not a lot out there, unfortunately. You're the first woman I've spent any time with and actually had a nice connection with. It's easy to talk to you. You're down-to-earth and real. Most people only show the image of themselves they want you to see...but you show everything. It's refreshing."

"Thanks..."

"I was engaged a few years ago. She was fooling around with my best friend. I had no idea. A few weeks before the wedding, she told me she wanted to be with him instead of me, and that was it. Haven't spoken to either one of them since."

"Wow... I'm so sorry."

"Don't feel bad for me," he said with a smile. "I'm glad we didn't get married and she just kept fooling around on me. It hurt at the time, but whatever. It's in the past now. I was heartbroken for a while. I really thought I was going to spend my life with this woman. And the betrayal of my best friend hurt just as much."

I felt so terrible for him.

"I tell you this story to give you hope. No matter how low you feel right now, you will get better. You'll fall in love again—with a much better man."

"How do you know?" I whispered.

He grinned. "Because I want that man to be me."

7

CONWAY

Vanessa was calling me.

I stared at her name on the screen as the dread filled up inside me. My sister never called me for a simple chitchat. It was always with a purpose. The phone rang exactly the same as it did any other time, but somehow, her rings sounded angry.

I sat on the couch in my bedroom and took the call. "Hey."

"Don't hey me," she snapped.

Yep. She knew.

"I've been trying to get a hold of Sapphire, but her phone isn't working. What's that about?"

No point in hiding it now. I couldn't lie to my sister, especially when it was pointless. The truth was going to come out at some point anyway.

"And why am I seeing her all over the news working for Lady Lingerie?" she snapped. "Con, did you guys break up?"

I closed my eyes for a brief moment, feeling sick to my stomach. "Yes."

"Yes what?" she asked. "You broke up?"

She was going to make me say it again? "Yes..."

"What?" she snapped. "Did she leave you for Andrew? Did she two-time you? Because I'll fly my ass to America and yank that pretty hair out of her—"

"It wasn't like that. I ended it."

Vanessa finally became quiet.

"It's a long story, but basically...she wanted more. I didn't."

Vanessa's silence was actually more terrifying than her words.

"She wanted to move to America to start over. That's why she's working for Andrew now."

"Con, you've got to be fucking kidding me right now. That woman was perfect. Are you out of your goddamn mind? You really think you can do better?"

"No." I know I couldn't.

"That woman was so good to you. Mom, Dad, and I loved her. How could you not see a future with her? Why did you ask her to move in with you in the first place if you didn't see it going anywhere?"

"It's not that simple…"

"Maybe I need to make it simple for you so you'll understand. Con, you're an idiot."

I listened to my sister berate me, a grown-ass man. "It doesn't matter. It's over now."

"You're making a huge mistake."

"Just stay out of it."

"How can I stay out of it? Sapphire is a great person."

"You hardly knew her."

"But I knew she loved you—and that's all that mattered.

When I saw the way she looked at you, like you were the only man on this planet, I knew we would be good friends. Because even if she were high-maintenance, annoying, or whatever, I wouldn't have cared. She loved you, and that was good enough for me to be friends with her. All those other skanks you hang around only care about your wallet, Con. Sapphire didn't."

I bowed my head and rubbed my fingers across my eye.

"Is it because she went on camera and said she loved you?"

I stayed quiet.

She sighed into the phone. "She wore her heart on her sleeve, Con. I think that's brave. If you don't, you didn't deserve her anyway."

Click.

CARTER SAT BESIDE ME AT THE BAR, DRINKING HIS whiskey and looking at the girls dancing in the background. In nothing but thongs, they worked the poles and danced for the cash men stuffed into their panties.

I hardly paid attention to them.

Carter didn't mention Muse anymore. He'd finally laid off it and moved on.

It was a relief, but it was also depressing.

Carter eyed two women sitting together at a table. Cosmos were sitting in front of them, and they both wore tight black dresses. It wasn't clear why they were hanging out in a strip joint, but judging by the way they made eyes at us, we were on their radar. "What do you think their story is?" Carter asked without looking at me, somehow knowing I was looking at them too.

"No idea. Maybe they're into perverts that come into a joint like this."

"You know that would make us perverts, by your logic."

"I don't think that statement is incorrect."

I drank my scotch again and watched them walk over to us. Both brunettes.

"I got the one on the right."

I didn't care which one I got stuck with.

They joined us at the bar, and the girls made small talk

with us as the music played overhead. The one near me played with my tie when she got comfortable, and she pressed closer into me, as if she was looking for a hard-on in my slacks.

She would be disappointed.

She finally called me out on my coldness. "I'm dropping moves left and right, but you're responding like a wall."

I'm not hard like a wall.

Carter was busy making out with his girl, so he wasn't listening to us anymore.

"I just got out of a relationship..."

She continued to spin my expensive tie around her fingers. "First time out, then?"

"Basically."

"Breakups are hard," she said. "But the sooner you get on top of someone, the sooner you move on. You want to get on top of me tonight?"

I didn't like her forwardness—it was too brash. "I'm happy to buy you a few drinks—but that's it."

"Or maybe start with a bathroom blow job?"

I didn't think any woman as attractive as her would be handing out sex and blow jobs that easily. She must know exactly who I was. She must know Muse was gone, and she wanted to be the woman to replace her. I could just fuck her mouth and walk away—but I still wasn't turned on.

If Muse asked to suck my dick in the bathroom stall, I'd be all over that.

But with some random woman...it wasn't appealing.

Carter wrapped his arm around his woman and took her out of the club, probably heading back to his place for a great night of meaningless sex.

Now all I wanted to do was go home—alone.

Dante knocked on my office door. "Sir?"

I was staring at the screen of my laptop, but I wasn't actually doing anything productive. She'd been gone for nearly two months now. It'd been seven weeks and three days—to be exact.

And I still wasn't over her.

I didn't stop thinking about her.

I didn't stop jerking off to her photos.

I didn't sleep with other women, staying just as monogamous as I was before.

What the fuck? How did she do this to me?

How did she change my life so drastically?

My life used to be so simple.

Now, it was nothing short of complicated. "I'm not hungry, Dante." My waist was getting smaller with every single week because my appetite hadn't returned.

"Actually, Mr. Barsetti is here to see you."

"Which one?" There were too many Mr. Barsettis in my family.

"Your father. Shall I send him up?"

My father never stopped by unannounced. It was obvious Vanessa told him what happened between Muse and me, and now he was coming by to check on me. A phone call wouldn't suffice because he couldn't see my face.

My father was the kind of man who would drive five hours just to see me for five minutes. "Send him in."

"Will do." He shut the door.

I closed my laptop and put it in the drawer before I broke out the scotch. I poured two glasses then moved to the two couches in the room. The walls of my office were surrounded by two enormous bookshelves stuffed with books. But honestly, it was just for decoration because I couldn't remember the last time I touched a book. I leafed through fashion magazines for inspiration sometimes.

My father stepped inside a few minutes later, dressed in black jeans, an olive green V-neck, and a black leather jacket. Fall had crept into the land, and now it wasn't warm like before. The wind had started to get cold, and the golden fields had started to turn green from the rain.

I didn't look up at him as he walked in. I wasn't being disrespectful. I just didn't have the energy.

He sat across from me and eyed the glass of scotch.

"I can get ice if you want."

He took a long drink before he set it down again. "You know why I'm here."

"I have a hunch." I rubbed my fingers across the coarse hair of my face. I didn't shave anymore, so I practically had a beard. Physical presentation didn't seem important to me anymore. I hardly left the house, and when I went to the studio in Milan, I didn't give a damn how I looked.

My father leaned back against the couch and crossed his legs, resting one ankle on the opposite knee. "Vanessa told your mother and me about Sapphire a few weeks ago. I thought I would give you some space to see if you'd talk about it on your own...but it doesn't seem like that's going to happen."

"There's nothing to say." I leaned back and rested my arm on the armrest.

"You're right. The beard and the dead look in your eyes tell me everything I need to know." My father wasn't afraid to dish out the truth—even if it stung a little. "Is this really what you want? You look like shit."

"Fuck you."

My father kept his cool, but the second he narrowed his eyes, the entire room shifted. It was suddenly darker, colder. His hostility lowered the temperature, making it ice-cold and unbearable. He had the kind of power I couldn't fathom, the ability to project so much emotion without saying a single word—or moving a finger.

I apologized before he retaliated. "I'm sorry...I shouldn't have said that."

He leaned forward and grabbed his drink again. He eyed me coldly as he downed the entire contents. He slammed it down on the wood a little harder. "I'm not going to be around forever, Conway. And when I'm not, that moment will haunt you for the rest of your life. So don't apologize. You'll pay for it later."

And just like that, my father made me feel like complete shit.

"This is what I see," he said as he poured himself another drink. "When Sapphire is around, you hit the peaks of your success. You're happy. You're relaxed, carefree. You even smile...once in a while. And now that she's gone, you haven't produced new pieces, you've stopped shaving, and you look like a man who's lost everything. I don't need to hear you say anything to know you're absolutely, undeniably miserable."

I grabbed my glass and nursed my wounds with a long drink of the aged scotch. I welcomed the burn down my throat and into my belly. That fire was the only warmth I had since Sapphire left.

"I didn't want to settle down and get married either, Conway. I fantasized about being a lifelong bachelor. Even after I met your mother, I didn't want things to change. I preferred being with different women because it didn't make me accountable for my actions. I could use them, hurt them, and dump them—without a hint of remorse."

My father had never told me such details of his life. I assumed he'd been promiscuous and reckless when he was young, based on the pieces I'd put together—along with Uncle Cane's stories.

"I never wanted to be a husband. I never wanted to be a father. But when your mother walked into my life, I had no other choice. I didn't want her to be with anyone else, and I didn't want to be with anyone else. There was no other way of life that would give me both. So I married her. I settled down. I sacrificed my previous life to have a new one with her. In the beginning, I dreaded it. But then I realized that simplicity was beautiful. And now...I wish I'd met her sooner."

I stared at my drink.

"Change is scary. But necessary."

"Why are you telling me this?" I asked. "It's over. She's living in New York now. I'm here. It's done."

"You still have time to fix this, Conway."

I refilled my glass.

"You love this woman. Don't let her end up with someone else. We only get one great woman our entire lives. If you think you have a chance of finding someone who makes you feel like this, it's not going to happen."

"What about there being other fish in the sea?" I countered.

"There are other fish in the sea," he said. "There will always be other fish in the sea. But they won't be bigger, brighter, or rarer. You'd rather bring home a different woman you won't remember every single night than have the best sex of your life with the same woman?"

Now we'd just stepped into new territory. "We aren't talking about my personal life. It's none of your business."

"It is my business when you're fucking it up. Trust me, I

don't want to talk about this any more than you do. But I can't let my son make the biggest mistake of his life."

"You don't know her…"

"I know her enough," he said quietly. "I know she makes you better. And that's all I need to know. She could be a prostitute, and that wouldn't make a difference to me. The only thing I care about is that you have someone to love you when your mother and I are gone."

"Stop saying that," I snapped. "I don't want to think about that right now…"

"It's going to happen, son. It could happen today, tomorrow, or in twenty years. You need to have your own family."

"I have Vanessa. I have—"

"It's not the same thing. A wife is different. If you'd never found anyone you loved, that would be different. But you have met someone…so don't let her go. Don't push her away just because you're afraid to commit. You're worried how it'll affect your work?" he asked incredulously. "Take a look at how her absence is affecting you now. You haven't worked in over a month."

"Are you keeping tabs on me now?"

"Always." He gripped his glass without taking a drink. "I always have tabs on you. Not because I'm spying—but because I care."

"No, that's the definition of spying."

"Shut up, Con. That's not what this conversation is about."

I couldn't tell him to shut up, but he could tell me to shut up all he wanted. Annoying.

"Make this right, Conway. Before someone else wins her over."

I didn't want to picture her with someone else. Just knowing someone was photographing her in nothing but her lingerie pissed me off. I missed having her around the house, a secret I got to cherish alone. "There's something you should know...and it's going to make you hate me a little bit."

My father set down his glass, and his eyes narrowed. "There's nothing you could say to make me hate you."

"Think again."

"No," he said firmly. "You could tell me you murdered someone, and I would still be sitting right here. That's unconditional love, that's what families do. I'm your father, and I will love you no matter what. So tell me."

I couldn't look at him as I spoke. "Sapphire came to me because she was on the run from a psychopath. He killed her brother, and he expected her to pay her brother's debt. The state took away the house she lost, so she had no way to pay him off. So he said he wanted her instead. She bought a plane ticket to Milan and auditioned for my show. She asked to be paid under the table, and I agreed."

He hung on every word.

"We worked together for a while, and she never told me about the asshole that was chasing her. The longer I worked with her, the more I felt inspired by her beauty. That's when my obsession started. I don't sleep with my models, and that's a policy I've never broken...but I couldn't stop imagining her in all these different scenarios..." I didn't feel strange telling my father this, not when he was going to break my face at the end of the conversation anyway. "Long story short, she was captured by the Skull Kings and brought to the Underground. I happened to be there for business, and her stalker was also there. We got into a bidding war... and I paid a hundred million to get her out of there. I took her to my place, and I told her she belonged to me exclusively. She was my prisoner, my muse. When you first met her, I told her to stay in my bedroom. But she snuck out and introduced herself as my girlfriend...and you adored her. She used it as leverage against me, said if I didn't treat her right, she would rat me out."

My father still didn't react, listening to every word.

"As time went on, things began to change. She became my friend, my confidant, my lover...and we were close. I shared my whole life with her. She shared hers with me. But I told her it didn't mean anything. I would never want marriage or a family. But then she told me she loved me...and that's when everything fell apart. I told her to leave...and that's the end of the story."

My father didn't move, even though I expected him to jump out of his seat and beat me senseless. At this point, I was in so much pain there was nothing he could do to make me feel worse. He could hit me if he wanted—and I would take it. He finally took a drink from his glass, lifting the tumbler high so he could get every drop in one gulp.

"Our relationship isn't what it seems...it's not real. It's just—"

"It's even more real," he said quietly. "Despite what you did to her, she still looked past the cruelty and fell in love with you. Con, that's how you know a woman's love is real. If she can accept you for who you are, all the good and all the bad, you know you met the right woman. And the second you want to be a better person for her... then you have to marry her."

"I'm surprised you aren't whacking me over the head with that scotch bottle..."

He tilted his face down slightly. "It would be hypocritical if I did..."

"What?" I whispered.

He leaned back into the couch, quiet as he considered his response. He rubbed his fingers across his chin, turning quiet. "Doesn't matter. This is your story, not mine. I can't stress it enough, Con. By doing nothing, you risk losing the love of your life. If you just tell her you're willing to work on it, that you love her, I know that will be enough for her to come back. But you have to meet her halfway."

I sighed under my breath.

He flashed me a look of disappointment. "When am I ever wrong about anything, son?"

I sighed again. "Never."

"Then answer this question—to yourself. She's been gone for seven weeks. With your newfound freedom and your bachelor lifestyle restored, how many women have you slept with?"

Did he know? My father might know a lot about my life, but there was no way to know who slept in my bed when the lights were off.

He gave me a knowing look, like he already knew the answer. "You don't want anything to change, but it already has. You're still in this relationship. You're still as committed as you ever were. So stop being in this relationship alone—get your damn woman back."

8

SAPPHIRE

OVER THE NEXT FEW WEEKS, I FINALLY FELL INTO A routine. New York started to feel like home, and while it didn't have the same beauty as Italy, it had a lot of its own good qualities. There was a coffee shop around the corner from my house that made the best coffee, so I stopped there every morning before I went to the gym. The park was a perfect place to jog, so when I didn't feel like breathing in the sweaty air from everyone around me, I took a trail through the trees. Now that fall had settled in, the leaves of the trees turned red and gold. My breath escaped as vapor in the cold mornings.

My life began to change, but one thing stayed the same.

Conway.

I still missed him.

I resented him for throwing us away. His work was more important than I would ever be, and holding on to pure, physical lust was better than intimate passion. Lust would always conquer love, and if I ever wanted him back, I would have to accept a loveless relationship.

But I couldn't pretend anymore.

This time, I knew he wasn't coming back. He came for me once, but when I didn't compromise, he got on his private jet and left me behind forever. I appreciated that he had been worried about me, especially after the way he'd kicked me out of his house in the middle of the night.

But now we were really over.

I went to the studio almost every day, and Andrew asked for my input on all of his designs. He kept hoping I'd absorbed some of Conway's genius so I would be able to pass it on to him, but even if I had, I would never share. I just told him things I liked, which fabrics hugged my skin better. We hadn't done a show yet, but he seemed to care more about photography, putting us in ads in magazines and in store windows.

When I saw my picture in the window of one of his lingerie shops in Manhattan, it was a little strange. It wasn't the same thing as looking in a mirror. My image had been changed a little, my appearance tweaked with a computer.

Nox and I hung out pretty often. He was my only friend in the city, and I enjoyed his company. He was easy to talk to, friendly, and super-hot. Sometimes we went for a walk in the park or grabbed dinner. He never tried to push for anything more, not after I told him how I felt about Conway. He never asked about him either.

After work one afternoon, we walked through the park as the sun started to set.

"Let's get our ten thousand steps in for the day then grab some food." He walked beside me in dark jeans and a long-sleeved deep blue shirt. The cold didn't seem to affect me as much as it affected him. Like Conway, Nox's built physique protected him from the cold. "Where do you want to go?"

"I have limited options, unfortunately." No carbs before bed. And nothing with too much fat or calories. Most of my dinners were comprised of fish and vegetables.

Salmon was packed with protein and nutrition, so that was my first choice. Ever since I'd changed my eating habits, I'd slimmed down almost immediately. The five pounds I was looking to lose came off within the first month. Now I was just maintaining.

"Man, that's hard. I couldn't do what you do."

"You have a strict diet too." He wouldn't look like that if he didn't watch what he ate.

"Yeah, but I have more wiggle room than you. I need calories. You're the opposite. Want to try that seafood place again?"

"If you don't mind."

He wrapped his arm around my shoulders, the affection playful more than romantic. "Of course, I don't mind. It's the price you pay when you're friends with a supermodel."

"I'm not a supermodel," I reminded him.

He scoffed. "Yes, you are. Come on, you're gorgeous. I can only name a few models off the top of my head, but you've sky-rocketed to celebrity almost instantly. And only supermodels do that."

Unfortunately, people recognized me when I went places. Sometimes people wanted a picture of me, and others wanted an autograph. I didn't consider myself to be a successful person, so I didn't know why people wanted those things, but I wasn't going to be rude and say no.

"How was work today?"

"Good. We're setting up a shoot in a disco bowling alley. A little different, but Andrew thinks it'll attract the attention of the average customer. Making it relatable, almost funny."

"That's cool. Will you be traveling anytime soon?"

"He hasn't mentioned any shows, so it doesn't seem like it. That's fine with me. I want to stay in one place for a while." The idea of traveling back to Milan sounded like a nightmare. I couldn't be in that city without being wrecked by emotion. "What did you do today?"

"I went to the gym in the morning, and then I played a few rounds of golf at the country club."

"I didn't know you golfed."

"I do pretty well. You wanna play sometime?" he asked.

"I've never golfed before."

"I can teach you."

We finished our walk through the park before we went to dinner. Anytime Nox and I hung out, we went out to dinner or the gym. He never invited me over, and I didn't either. Since we were just friends, it seemed like we should do stuff outside the house—not behind closed doors.

"So, how's Operation Get Over Conway?" he asked at the end of the meal.

I hadn't made much progress, which was discouraging because it'd been almost a month since I saw him. When I couldn't sleep at night, I touched myself and imagined he was there. I got off with my hand, whispering his name into the darkness of my bedroom. I was still sleeping with him—even though he wasn't there with me. He'd probably fucked dozens of other women by now. I should just sleep with Nox to expedite the process of moving forward, but I couldn't do that. It wasn't fair to Nox or me. "Honestly, nothing has really changed. I think about him pretty often."

If Nox was upset about that, he didn't act like it. "Do you still talk to him?"

"No. We've had no contact."

"It takes time. It took me about four months to really get over what happened with my fiancée. So, you still have a ways to go."

I was baffled that he wanted to keep waiting around for me. "That's two more months...you could find someone great in that amount of time."

The corner of his mouth rose in a smile. "I could get into my safety school right away because it was easy to get accepted right off the bat...or I could wait for the school that I really want. I'm first on the waitlist, right?"

"Well...you're the only person on the waitlist," I said with an awkward laugh.

"That's even better. So there's no rush. I like getting to know you anyway. You're a cool chick."

My lips automatically stretched into a smile. "You're great too, Nox. It's hard to believe I have this super-hot guy showing so much interest in me."

His eyebrows rose. "You think I'm hot? Not just hot, but super-hot?"

"Uh, duh. Look at you."

He grinned. "Well, thanks. I think you're super-hot too. Hopefully, we can be a super-hot couple soon..."

When we finished dinner, we split the tab like always and then headed to the sidewalk.

"Can I walk you home?" he asked. "Or better yet, you want to come over and watch a movie? It's only seven, unless you have work in the morning."

"I'm off tomorrow," I blurted.

"Is that a yes, then?" he asked.

Maybe I shouldn't go over there, but I'd told him I wasn't over Conway yet, so it shouldn't matter. We would just spend time together the way we'd already been doing. "Yeah. Sure."

WHEN I WENT TO WORK TWO DAYS LATER, ANDREW greeted me in his studio. His supplies lay on the table, and his lingerie piece was on the mannequin. "Sapphire, how was your day off?"

"Good." My body was wrapped in the silk robe he

provided for me, ready to put on his next piece. "How was yours?"

"My boys had baseball camp all day. Thankfully, the weather has cooled down. Otherwise, it would be unbearable." He felt the fabric in his hands before he set it aside. "Glad to see you're finally moving on."

I stared at him blankly, unsure what he meant by that. "Sorry?"

He grabbed the newspaper and handed it to me. "There's an article about you and the new guy you're seeing."

My fingertips immediately went numb, and when I grabbed the paper, I could barely feel it. I looked at the pictures, seeing one of us in the park, at the restaurant, and even walking into his apartment. We were smiling in almost every photograph, looking happy together like a couple in love. The article was longer than it should be, talking about the seriousness of our relationship and how Conway Barsetti was a thing of the past.

Being famous sucked.

I wondered what Conway would think if he saw this,

especially since it wasn't true, but then I realized it didn't matter.

He'd been with dozens of women already.

I was the one who took forever to finally move on.

9

CONWAY

My father's word sank deep into me, but I still didn't do anything about it.

I'd made my choice.

Another three weeks had passed, and I was just as miserable as I was before.

Nicole started to pressure me about new pieces, but I didn't have a single design ready. I still hadn't slept with anyone because jerking off to Muse was a lot more pleasurable than fucking a stranger. I stopped going out with Carter because I didn't want to bother making small talk with a woman I would never take home.

Vanessa was still pissed at me.

Marco was disappointed.

My entire life had been irrevocably changed. Muse affected so many people, and now that she was gone, people were angry. They missed her.

Fuck, I missed her.

Maybe my father was right. Maybe everyone was right.

But was it too late?

Carter stopped by in the middle of the day on Tuesday. He never did that because he was too busy with all of his business projects. But ever since Muse left, he checked on me. He tried to be discreet about it, but I knew exactly what he was doing.

He stepped inside my office, a newspaper tucked under his arm.

"Scotch?" I asked.

"It's ten."

"So?" I poured myself a glass, having no concept of time anymore. All I could truly sense was the rising and setting of the sun. I knew when it was daytime and when it was nighttime, but that was it.

He sat across from me then touched the newspaper with his fingertips.

I stared at him. "What is it, Carter?"

"I'm not sure if I should show this to you...or if it'll make any kind of a difference." He tossed the newspaper onto the table.

My eyes spotted Muse right away, but she wasn't alone.

She was with some six-foot-three good-looking guy. With blue eyes, a muscular physique, and a charming smile, he was the definition of a pretty boy. His arm was around her at the park, and then they were huddled close together over dinner. The last picture was the two of them entering his apartment on Park Avenue—so he was wealthy.

I already felt like shit, but this dragged me down to a whole new level.

Fuck.

She was seeing someone.

I scanned through the article and picked up on a few things. It discussed their relationship, that they'd been seen out together for the past month. He owned a few gyms, but other than that, they didn't have any other important information.

I turned it over and set it back on the table.

Carter stared at me, as if he waited for me to unleash my rampage.

I was sick to my stomach, weak, and dead inside. The jealousy I felt was something I'd never known before. It was powerful, terrifying, and sickening. I wanted to rip this guy's eyes out and feed them to a dog. I wanted to crush his skull underneath my shoe. I didn't give a damn how nice he was.

He wasn't good enough for her.

Carter shook his head slightly as he stared at me. "Looks like you waited too long."

I DIDN'T KNOW WHAT THE FUCK I WAS DOING.

Once the adrenaline set in, my heart pounded nonstop. I didn't sleep because I was too livid to feel tired. All I felt was pain, the kind of torture that made powerful men crack. I was devastated, so hurt I could barely suck in a breath.

I didn't think twice before I ordered my jet to be prepared for the voyage to New York.

I landed at three in the morning, when the city was the quietest—even though it never slept.

I didn't know what my purpose was, what I hoped to accomplish. If she was seeing this handsome guy, she'd obviously moved on from me. It's been almost three months in total since she sped off into the night in my Ferrari.

It wasn't like she didn't wait long enough.

But this still felt like a betrayal—a horrid heartbreak.

I should just go to the hotel and rest until morning, but I couldn't do that. I had to see her right that second. Maybe she was staying at her boyfriend's place, or better yet, he was staying at hers.

I'd love to come face-to-face with him.

And murder him.

I got into her building and arrived at her front door. I stared at the hardwood, debating whether I should do this or not. What was the purpose of this anyway? I couldn't get angry at her when she did nothing wrong. She didn't owe me anything, so this wasn't a betrayal. I was the one who broke her heart.

Not the other way around.

Even though I'd been killed in the process.

My finger hit the doorbell.

Now, all I had to do was wait. The damage had been done, and the ball was rolling.

I waited for a long time before I heard her footsteps hit the hardwood floor in her apartment. If she was dressed in just his t-shirt, I'd punch a hole through the wall. My hands tightened into fists just from thinking about it.

When her footsteps stopped, I knew she was standing at the door—looking through the peephole.

Looking at me.

The door cracked open, and her shocked expression looked into mine. Her eyebrows were high off her face, her skin was pale like milk, and her hair was pulled back into a loose bun. She kept one hand on the door as she looked at me, either because she was prepared to shut it in my face or she needed it for balance.

Now I had her attention. But I didn't know what to do with it.

"Conway...what are you doing here? It's almost four in the morning."

I invited myself inside and yanked the door from her grasp. I shut it behind me. "Is he here?" I stepped into her apartment and scanned the room, expecting to see a large, muscular man ready to rush me. If he was there, I'd be even angrier. How could he let her open the door by herself? Even if she lived in a nice building, this was still New York. Crazy shit happened every night.

"Who?"

I turned my fierce gaze on her. "Don't play that fucking game."

She crossed her arms over her chest, her gaze narrowing on my face. "If this is a joke, it's a bad one."

"Do you see me laughing?" Another sweep of the apartment told me there wasn't any sign of him, of his shoes kicked off on the rug or his jacket hanging from the back of a chair. He would have come out of the bedroom at the sound of our voices by now.

"Conway." She slowly crept into the living room, eyeing me with sheer disappointment. She was in a long t-shirt that reached her knees, covering her bottom. It was a man's t-shirt, and I wondered if it was his. "You're absolutely pathetic. I can't believe I ever respected you."

Like she'd punched me in the gut, I was winded.

"You break my heart and then have the nerve to throw a tantrum when I start seeing someone? Are you two? I don't owe you a goddamn thing, Conway. I told you I loved you and I wanted to marry you, but you left anyway. You have no right to be jealous. You have no right to show up on my doorstep at four in the morning huffing and puffing. Now get the fuck out of my apartment and don't come back."

I'd taken a bad situation and made it worse. Now she despised me even more. I'd waited too long to get my shit together, and I'd pushed away the one woman I adored. Now she was sleeping in someone else's arms.

Because I was a fucking idiot.

"Go, Conway." It was the second time she'd asked me to leave.

But I didn't move. I stayed still, feeling the searing pain across my heart. I wanted to be the man between her legs. I wanted to be the designer who used her for inspiration every day. I wanted her to live in my mansion, enjoying a life of luxury only I could provide. "I'm sorry—"

"I don't care. Please leave. I can't even look at you right now..." She stepped back, putting more distance between us. "I'll call the cops if I have to."

I ran my fingers through my hair, trying to think of the right thing to say. I didn't come here with a plan, so coming up with something on the spot was difficult. My chest swirled with emotions, but I couldn't articulate them. "Muse, let me tell you what my life has been like for the past three months."

She didn't ask me to leave again, but her guard was still up.

"I've been miserable." I slid my hands into my pockets. "The bed we used to sleep in together has never felt more uncomfortable. I hardly sleep. I don't eat. Dante is constantly trying to shove food down my throat because

I'm getting thinner by the week. Nicole is pestering me to submit a new line of designs, but I haven't sketched a single idea. I spend my nights with my scotch and stare at the fireplace. I think of you constantly. My father told me to get my shit together and get you back, but I was too stubborn to listen. Vanessa is pissed at me. Carter thinks I'm an idiot. My whole world has fallen apart since you've been gone. There hasn't been anyone else..." I watched the way her eyes changed, the slight look of relief. "I've gone out with the intention of picking up a random woman, but I always go home alone. I jerk off to the lingerie pictures of you I see in magazines..." I felt like a teenage boy doing it, but it was still better than fucking a stranger. I should feel ashamed for saying the truth out loud, but I didn't. "I keep telling myself this is the only option, but this option has left me devastated. When Carter showed me the article with you and...him, something snapped inside me. It kills me to see you with someone else. It kills me because...I miss you so goddamn much."

She tilted her head slightly as she examined me, the ferocity slowly fading away.

"I don't know what I expected to accomplish by coming here tonight. But...I wasn't thinking."

The silence fell between us, and she kept staring at me like she was waiting for me to say something else.

But that was it. I had nothing else to say.

"What do you want, Conway?" she whispered. "Do you want me to pack up my things and fly home with you right now?"

It would be a dream come true. "Yes."

"Well, you know what I want. That hasn't changed." She stared at me with her pretty eyes, pressuring me to say the words she wanted to hear.

I held her gaze but remained silent.

"You still won't give me what I want..."

I already knew how I felt about her. It was perfectly clear. I could keep fighting it, but that hadn't gotten me anywhere. The last three months had been wasted in a painful depression. I'd never been so low in my life. I was happy before this woman walked into my life, but now that she was gone, I couldn't find happiness again.

Because she was my happiness.

I walked across the room toward her, my hands shaking with anticipation. It'd been so long since I'd held her, so long since I'd touched her. I missed those lips against mine. I missed the way her fingers glided through my hair when I made love to her. I missed having my woman beside me in bed every single night.

I stopped in front of her and slid my hand under the fall of her hair. I felt her stiffen at my touch, felt her breathing quicken once we were connected again. She didn't pull away, but I could still see the trepidation in her eyes. I'd hurt her so many times, and now she was afraid I would hurt her again. "I don't want to love you. I don't want to feel this way. I don't want to sit around my house and think about our trip to Greece. I don't want to touch myself to the memory of you when I want the real thing. I don't want you to have this power over me, this hold over my happiness. If I could, I would forget about you and fill my bed with women I'll never remember. But I can't...because you're a part of me now. Even when you've been on the other side of the world, I've been committed to you. I've worried about you. I've dreamed about you, wished you were mine again. So I can't keep lying to myself anymore. I can't keep lying to you—to the entire world." Both of my palms cupped her cheeks, and I forced her gaze on me, our eyes connected in intensity. "I love you, Muse. I've loved you since the moment I laid eyes on you. You became my muse, my obsession, and then the love of my life. So please, tell me you still love me. Tell me I'm not too late."

She closed her eyes for a brief moment, the corners of her mouth rising in a smile. When she opened her eyes again, the moisture had coated their surface, and now the tears dripped down her face. "It's never too late, Conway. Not with you."

My hands gripped her tighter, and the pain that had clutched my heart for months released at last. I pressed my forehead to hers and finally felt at peace. I felt my hands stop shaking. I felt the wounds in my heart turn to scar tissue. I'd dreaded this moment for so long, but now that it was finally here, it was euphoric.

It felt right.

"I love you too, Conway."

I grabbed her t-shirt and pulled it over her head, revealing nothing but her skin. I tossed the shirt on the ground, wanting her to never have anything to do with that pretty boy ever again. She belonged to me, and if that asshole came anywhere near her, I'd kill him. "End it with him. And throw his shit out."

Instead of flinching at my hostility, she smiled.

"What?"

"That's your shirt, Conway. Not his."

My eyes narrowed on hers, feeling a surge of relief run through me. "You're still wearing my shirts to bed?"

"I've always worn your shirts to bed."

I pulled her hips into me and kissed her, melting into her deep embrace. It was the affection I'd been missing, the affection I lived for. It made me feel alive, gave me more joy than all of my success. She was mine again, and I would make sure I never had to live without her.

Because I'd rather be dead than live without her again.

I LAY BESIDE HER IN BED. STRIPPED DOWN TO MY boxers, I held her tightly against me. She had a queen-sized bed, and her master bedroom held the elegance of a queen. In shades of pink and white, it complemented her presence perfectly.

My fingers moved through her hair as I stared at her, examining the softness of her features. As much as I wanted to be buried between her legs, I knew that was off-limits for the night. "Break up with him in the morning."

"It is morning."

"Then break up with him now."

Her fingers moved down my hard chest. "I'm not sure if I should tell you this or not…"

"What?" I whispered.

"Well…I was never dating Nox—"

"I don't want to hear his name."

Her smile widened. "So jealous…I like it."

I hated it.

"I was never dating him. I haven't even kissed him, Conway."

My eyes narrowed, and my sense of relief was flooded with confusion. "What does that mean?"

"He asked me out a month ago, but I told him I wasn't ready to date. So we've been hanging out as friends. He said he was willing to wait until I was over you."

Because he knew she was a serious catch. Even if she

was in love with another guy, she was still a goddess. I would have done the same thing. "So you've never slept with him?"

"No."

"Or kissed him?"

"No. The most he's ever done is wrap his arm around my shoulder."

I growled.

She chuckled in my face. "Get over yourself, Con."

So this woman was still mine. She'd always been mine. I flew across the world because my jealousy clouded my judgment. I came to claim my woman so no one else could have her. It was reckless and stupid, but perhaps I needed to be reckless and stupid.

"If I'd known all I had to do to get you over here was make you jealous, I would have done something a long time ago."

And I wished she had. "Then you've always been mine."

"Always, Con."

I rolled on top of her, watching her eyes light up as I

separated her legs. My hard cock pressed against her body through my boxers and her panties. I ground against her slowly, watching her eyes darken in arousal.

Her fingers slowly slid through my hair, and she stared at my lips, waiting for a kiss.

I hadn't been with her in so long that I knew my performance would be laughable. I already wanted to come just from grinding against her. The shape of her mouth made my cock harden. The pretty look in her eyes made me twitch. Everything about her got me rock-hard.

Not to mention the fact that I loved her.

She reached for my boxers and tugged them down, letting my big cock come free. "Make love to me, Conway."

My balls tightened against my body, and a quiet growl escaped my lips.

"And tell me you love me at the same time." She pulled her panties down her thighs then pushed them to her ankles. Then she spread her legs for me again, parting them wide so she could take me.

Fuck.

I moved on top of her and watched her lie back on the pillow. My crown oozed with my arousal, and I could barely breathe knowing how slick her pussy was at that moment. Three months of jerking off to a woman I lost made me painfully horny. Instead of picking up some random woman who wouldn't satisfy me, I'd pretended this woman was still mine.

And now I would finally have her.

I pressed the head of my cock inside her and slowly slid through her slickness. She was exceptionally tight, like I was breaking her in again. She hadn't been fucked in months, and now she was tight like a virgin.

She was mine to claim all over again.

I moved until I was completely inside, my entire body shaking because she felt so good. She bit her bottom lip as she stared up at me, her face flushing from the pleasure.

She widened her legs farther and then yanked on my hips, pulling me deeper inside her. "Conway..."

I pressed my forehead to hers and breathed with her, treasuring the way our bodies fit together so well. My cock had made a home between her legs—

and he never wanted to leave. It was so good, so tight.

I already wanted to come. "I'm not gonna last…"

"Neither am I." She gripped my shoulders. "I miss feeling your come inside me."

I groaned in her face, my cock twitching in reaction. "Muse…"

She tugged on my hips, getting me to thrust.

I rocked into her slowly, moving at the slowest speed I ever had. After three months of abstinence, just a little bit of friction with her was more than enough. She felt like a virgin, but so did I.

She gripped my ass and pulled me into her, showing the same enthusiasm. She kept biting her bottom lip and moaning, like she was crumbling apart just the way I was. She breathed in my face, sexy whimpers escaping her throat. "Tell me you love me."

It had been hard to say it the first time, but it wasn't hard to say it the second time. "I love you."

Her nails dug into my back as she exploded, coming all around me in a violent orgasm. She whimpered in my face, her slickness coating my cock all the way to the hilt. We barely moved for a minute, and we were coming apart like teenagers.

I came immediately afterward, and I was grateful she went first. If she hadn't, I would have left her unsatisfied. I shoved my dick as far as I could go and released, dumping all of my come inside that tight little cunt.

My cunt.

She moaned with me even though she'd finished her climax. "I love you..."

The words only made my orgasm better, stronger.

I filled her with all my come and felt my cock soften afterward. I released more than I ever had before, and the sensation was so strong, I felt all the muscles in my shoulders tense. I used to have this every single night of my life, but then I turned my back and let it slip away.

I wouldn't make that mistake again.

WHEN I WOKE UP THE NEXT DAY, MUSE WAS ALREADY wide awake. She'd already showered, had breakfast, and now she was reading beside me, scrolling through a novel on her tablet. She was in black leggings and a long-sleeved shirt, dressed for fall.

I squinted my eyes and stared at her alarm clock.

It was three in the afternoon.

Jesus.

I was always up by seven. With the time change, the lack of sleep, jet lag, and a night catching up on good sex, I was knocked out.

I rubbed the sleep from my eyes and groaned. "Shit...it's late."

She set down her tablet and turned over to face me. "It's okay to sleep in once in a while. Or, for the first time ever, in your case."

Even when we were in Greece, I was up early in the morning. I took care of emails and did my daily sit-ups and push-ups before I watched the sun rise. I propped myself on my elbow and looked down at Muse. I missed waking up to her face first thing in the morning. I preferred to see her when her face was free of makeup, and her skin was beautiful from resting all night. But she was still absolutely stunning. "This feels like a dream."

"But better, because it's real." She leaned down to kiss me on the mouth.

My lips moved with hers, and the tightness in my chest slipped away. My hand slid into her hair, and I smelled her perfume. I'd fantasized about the smell, treasured it as it remained glued to my sheets. Once that smell had faded away, I'd felt like I lost her all over again.

"Want some breakfast?" she asked.

"You cook?"

"Yes." She gave me a playful slap on the arm. "You would know that if Dante let me do something once in a while."

"You know how he is. The proudest man I know."

She released a loud scoff. "Maybe one of them. But definitely not the proudest."

I followed her out of the bedroom, dressed in my boxers and the t-shirt I wore yesterday. She had two large couches and one armchair on a colorful rug. A large TV was on the wall. There were paintings hanging, all of them images of Italy.

I knew that wasn't a coincidence.

She grabbed her ingredients out of the fridge and the pantry and started to cook at the counter.

"Need help?"

"Nope." She poured me a fresh mug of coffee.

I sipped it as I watched her move in the kitchen. She made pancakes on the stove, baked the bacon in the oven, and whipped up scrambled eggs. Within ten minutes, she served me a meal full of carbs, fat, and sugar.

I hadn't had a breakfast like this in years. "I'm surprised you had all this around the house."

"I went to the store when you were asleep." She sat in the seat perpendicular to me, her hair curled and earrings in her lobes. She was thinner since the last time I saw her. Andrew must have asked her to drop a few extra pounds. Unless she was just depressed and didn't eat.

I ate everything on my plate, loving the fluffy cakes and even the syrup. The bacon was crispy, just the way I liked it. When it came to Muse, I always felt the urge to take care of her, to make sure my chef made the food she liked and picked out the clothes she wanted. I'd never had a woman take care of me before. I was perfectly capable of making my own food, but it was entertaining to watch her do it.

Watch her do something for me.

The second I was reunited with her, I felt better. Like I'd been in a desert for three months, I was dehydrated, sick, and losing my mind. But now I was refreshed, getting everything I needed to nurse me back to health.

Her plate was mediocre, a single pancake, half a slice of bacon, and scrambled egg whites. I preferred to see her eat a real meal. Andrew wanted her to be as slim as possible, but thinner wasn't necessarily better. I liked seeing a little stomach on her, more meat on her thighs. I wanted her to come home with me so she could eat all she wanted.

Like a real woman.

I pushed my plate away and adjusted my position in my chair so I could face her better, so I could watch her put the small bites into her mouth. This was one of the things I missed most, having the privilege of staring at her during all my meals. She was far more entertaining than a TV program or a piece of art.

She smiled slightly when she became aware of my stare. "Some things never change, huh?"

"No." I propped my elbow on the table and rested my chin against my fingertips. "We'll return home tomorrow. That should give you the afternoon to tell Andrew you're leaving."

She stopped chewing, her mouth still full. She paused as she stared at me, and she quickly finished chewing before she forced the food down her throat. "What?"

"Do you need a few more days?" I could have someone handle selling her place while we were away. There was nothing she couldn't take with her. All the furniture in her apartment could go on my plane.

"No...I just...wasn't expecting you to say that."

"Say what, exactly?"

She set down her silverware. "Well, I can't leave, Conway."

My eyes narrowed, immediately annoyed by that disgusting sentence. "What does that mean?"

"I work here. I live here. I can't just drop everything and leave."

"I know you can't do that immediately. That's why I recommended you take a few days."

"You don't get it," she whispered. "I signed a contract with Andrew for ten years. I can't just walk away."

"You can always walk away. Contracts are broken all the time."

"Well, I can't break this one."

My body automatically went rigid, the mere suggestion that some man had a stronger claim over her than I did was insulting. "Why not?"

"I have to pay back what I owe. I already bought this place and all the furniture."

"Don't worry about that, Muse. I'll take care of it."

When her eyes narrowed, she showed her displeasure. "I don't need you to pay my debts, Conway."

I forgot how proud she was. "Then what do you suggest?"

She fell quiet, knowing there was no other option. She would have to get a job doing something else if she ever wanted to pay back every cent she'd received.

"Then let me take care of it," I said gently. "The contract will be over, and you can come back with me."

When she avoided my gaze, I knew there was something wrong.

"What is it, Muse?"

"I...I don't want to go back to what we were."

My fingertips moved over my lips.

"I don't want to be so dependent on you. When you were pissed off, you threw me out on the street."

I cringed, hating myself for that stupid impulse.

"Fortunately, Andrew had already offered me that deal. If I hadn't had that on the table, I have no idea what I would have done."

"That suitcase had three hundred thousand dollars in it. The Ferrari is worth over two fifty."

"But I've never wanted your money, Conway. How many times do I have to say it?"

I felt her emotional stare burrow right under my skin.

"Unless I have something more secure, I need my own

income. I need my own independence. So I need to keep this job and my apartment."

My eyebrows shot up. "You can't be serious."

"I am serious, Con."

Just when I thought everything was perfect, it went to shit. "We can't have a long-distance relationship."

"Well…"

"I'm not doing that." I tried to keep my temper under control, but it was already rising. I knew exactly what I wanted, and I wouldn't settle for less. I told this woman I loved her. It was the first time I'd said it to anyone. I wasn't going to live on the other side of the world away from her. "You're sleeping in my bed every night. You're living under my roof."

"We can still do that, but here. You work remotely most of the time anyway."

I was tempted to slam my fist against her dining table. "Muse, you know how much my family means to me. I can't live that far away from them. It doesn't make any sense for us to live here just for you to have a job."

"The only way around it is if I have a job there."

"Fine," I said. "You can work for me. Problem solved."

She shook her head. "I can't work for you, Conway."

"Why the hell not?"

"Because all you have to do is get pissed off and I'm out of a job."

I rolled my eyes. "Muse, a night like that isn't going to happen ever again. I came all the way here to tell you I love you and to bring you back home with me. It's different now. Let's go back to Verona and live in that beautiful mansion you love so much that's way too big for a single person, alright?"

Her eyes drifted toward the table. "I'm sorry...but no. I need more than that."

"More than that?" I asked incredulously.

"It would be different if we were married. But for right now, this is how it has to be. We've never had a real relationship. It's always been in a situation where you have power over me. I want my own place—"

"I'm not letting you live alone. Nonnegotiable. I need you in a place where I know you're safe, and there's no place in the world safer than beside me. As for marriage...don't push me. It was hard enough for me to come all the way here and put my heart on the line. It was hard enough to admit how much I need you. Let's start there and see where it goes..."

"So marriage is on the table?"

It was a step I'd never thought I would take, but I'd also thought I would never love someone the way I loved her. Like my father said, this kind of commitment had already happened—whether I chose to acknowledge it or not. "All I know is...I can't live without you. So yes, it's on the table."

"And children?" she whispered. "You know I have to have a family...since I don't have one of my own."

I could barely grasp the idea of being a husband. A father was even more terrifying. "I'm not ready for that right now. But...it's on the table."

She released a quiet sigh. "That's enough for me."

It was all of me, so it better be enough for her. "So you'll live with me?"

"I guess. But I still need a job."

I growled under my breath. "I'll just give you—"

"I don't want your money."

I loved this woman, but damn, she was infuriating. "Look, I'm pretty fucking helpless without you. I haven't made a single sketch since you walked out on me. I'm behind schedule, and I'm drowning. People are waiting for me to reveal something new, but I can't even produce a single concept. So I need you. Being my muse is a job. It's a damn important one. I'm willing to pay you what Andrew is paying you—because my entire career depends on you."

"Like I said, I don't want—"

"I know. But if you were someone else, I'd be paying you. If you think about it like that, it's a job. So you're helping me, and I'm helping you."

"I still owe you a hundred million."

"You don't owe me anything, Muse."

"No. If you really want to do it this way, I want to pay you back for what you spent on me."

It wasn't ideal, but we were moving in the right direction. "So if I offered to match what Andrew is paying you—"

"You would deduct the hundred million you paid, plus the cost to break me out of the contract."

"That's about one hundred and forty million..."

"Yes."

I felt like an ass taking anything from her.

"That would leave the rest for me to keep. I would hold on to it, and if we do get married someday, I can give it back to you...since there's no point in me keeping it anymore."

It was the best scenario we were going to compromise on. She earned her own money that she could rely on, and in the event that she didn't need it, which she wouldn't, she would just give it back to me. It would allow her to work with me every day without being a public figure, and she could be with me at all times.

Win-win.

"I think we have a deal," I said.

"Yeah. I think we do."

HAND IN HAND, WE WALKED INTO THE STUDIO WHERE Muse spent her afternoons working with Andrew. They had a photo set on one floor, the fabrics on a different level, and they had a special gym where the models could work out if they wanted to.

We took the elevator to one of the upper floors, where Andrew had his office.

His secretary told us to have a seat, so we waited together in the lobby.

I sat beside her in my black suit, my legs apart and my eyes fierce. Andrew wouldn't let her go without a fight. His standing in the market had exploded since Muse started working for him. The sales started to pour in, and once she was gone, they would plummet all over again.

He would be pissed.

My phone started to ring, and if my father's name hadn't been on the screen, I wouldn't have answered it. "I'll be right back." My hand slid from Muse's thigh as I stood up and approached the double glass doors. I passed through then took the call. "Hey, everything alright?"

My father spoke with a calm and cool voice. "I have the same question for you. I stopped by the house, but Dante said you left for the airport a few days ago. Said you were headed to New York..."

"Yeah. I'm still here."

"May I ask what you're doing? Keep in mind, there's only one answer I'm looking for."

I grinned then walked back into the waiting room. "Hold on." I sat beside Muse and handed her the phone. "Say hello to my father."

She smiled before she took the phone. "Mr. Barsetti, how are you?"

I could hear his voice over the line. He instantly seemed to be in a much better mood talking to her instead of me. "Sapphire, I'm doing great...really great. It's nice to hear your voice again."

"It's nice to hear yours too."

"I'm glad my son manned up."

"Yeah," she said with a chuckle. "Me too."

"When you guys get back to town, Pearl and I would love to see you. We were disappointed when we heard the two of you were no longer seeing each other. Vanessa took it the hardest."

"I would love that. Maybe we can do dinner..."

"Definitely," he said. "Well, I'll let you go."

"Do you want to talk to Con again?"

I held out my hand to take the phone.

"Nope." He hung up.

She couldn't hide her grin as she dropped the phone into my hand. "Must be busy..."

I stuffed the phone into my pocket, knowing my father was just resentful toward me after our last conversation. "I told him the truth about us."

"The truth?" She raised an eyebrow. "What does that mean?"

"The whole truth. He knows how we met. He knows I bought you from the Underground. He knows everything."

"Oh...it seems like he took it well."

"He didn't give me too much shit about it. I thought he was going to smash the bottle of scotch over my head and knock me out, but he didn't. He probably thought it was pointless since I was already so miserable. Not much he could do to make me feel worse."

She moved her hand to my thigh.

"But the truth is out."

"I guess it's nice we don't have to pretend anymore. It's easy to live under the light of the truth instead of the shadow of a lie."

Andrew's assistant approached us then guided us into his office. "Mr. Lexington is ready to see you now."

The second I looked at Andrew's face, I knew he was pissed. And he knew exactly why I was there. Like the last time we met, we didn't shake hands. I sat in one of the chairs facing him, giving him a silent greeting.

Muse spoke to him with the same warmth she spoke to everyone. "Hello, Andrew. Thanks for meeting with us."

He was cold to her, but not nearly as cold as he was to me. "Sure. I think I know why you're here." He turned to me. "Sapphire is under contract, as I'm sure you know. The only way to break that is with cash—so I hope you brought your checkbook."

"Of course," I said. "Sapphire will be returning with me

to Italy. So your arrangement ends today."

He turned his gaze back to her. "I hope you're sure about this. Because if there's another bump in the road, there won't be a home for you here." It was a subtle threat, but a threat nonetheless. He couldn't persuade her to stick around, not while I was in the room. That was all he had at his disposal.

But Muse didn't flinch. "I understand, Andrew. Thank you for everything you've done for me. I appreciate it. I know Conway is a bit quiet, but I know he appreciates how well you treated me."

"Because he didn't treat you right himself," Andrew said coldly.

My hand tightened into a fist, but I didn't rise to the challenge. I couldn't combat his comment when it was absolutely true. When I threw Muse off my property, it was the dumbest decision I had ever made.

I wouldn't fuck up like that again.

I'd do everything I could to keep her around.

"Let's crunch those numbers now." I pulled my checkbook out of my pocket along with a pen. "And we'll be on our way."

10

SAPPHIRE

ITALY WASN'T THE SAME AS IT WAS WHEN I LEFT.

Now it was cold, cloudy, and wet. The sun was blocked by thick clouds, so the fields didn't shine with the same splashes of green and gold. The heat that I adored had disappeared, and I wondered how long it would be before it returned.

We got into the SUV at the airport, and his men drove us back to his place in Verona.

Conway sat beside me, holding my hand on his thigh. He'd hung up his suit during the flight and put it back on once the plane landed on the runway. Dressed for anything and everything, Conway projected the same intense confidence whether he was traveling or not.

He turned his face toward me, watching me examine the surroundings through the window. "There's just a storm passing through. October is a beautiful month here. Once we hit November, the temperature will drop, and we'll start to get snow."

"So the sun will come back?" I asked hopefully.

"Yeah. It'll be here for a few more weeks. Then we'll have to move the horses and everything in the barn."

"Good idea."

We drove for another twenty minutes before we approached the gates to his mansion. Three stories and beautiful, it was still stunning just like I remembered. I stared as it came closer into view, seeing the ivy along the walls and the fountain still pouring water. Joy filled my heart the second I looked at it. I never felt this way when I returned to New York. I'd lived there my whole life, but I didn't have this same kind of affection for it.

But this place was different.

He leaned into me and brushed his lips against my forehead. "Welcome home."

MY CLOTHES WERE ORGANIZED IN THE CLOSET. ALL the things I was forced to leave behind were still there. My hair and makeup supplies were in the bathroom drawer, and the top drawer in the dresser was filled with my panties and lingerie.

It'd been three months, so I'd assumed he would have thrown everything out.

"You kept everything."

"Of course." He slid his jacket off his arms and threw it over of the back of the chair. He removed his tie next and draped it across his jacket. The pieces of his outfit fell away one by one, until he was stripped down to just his black boxers.

He wasn't as thick as he used to be. The muscles in his arms weren't as well defined, and the sculpted grooves along his stomach weren't so deep. He hadn't put on weight, just lost muscle. Spending his time not eating and not exercising had changed his appearance.

The opposite had happened to me, because I was forced to.

"You want me to have Dante bring us dinner?"

My internal clock was off. It was evening here, but my

mind was still in daylight mode. I slept a lot on the plane, so I wasn't necessarily tired. But I wasn't hungry either. "No, I'm okay." I stripped off my clothes until I was just in my panties. And like no time had passed at all, I opened his drawer and searched for a clean shirt to wear. I stared at the pile of choices and smiled, realizing how some things never changed. I picked a white one and pulled it over my body, surrounded by the soft cotton that naturally smelled like him.

"Anything you want to do in particular? I would take you to see the horses, but it's dark and cold."

I pulled back the covers and got into my bed, the bed I was used to sleeping in. I lay back and felt the mattress and the sheets. It felt exactly the same as I remembered, so perfectly comfortable. Lying there felt like a dream. I'd imagined myself there so many times, my hand between my legs as I pictured him thrusting inside me. "I just want to lie here...I missed this bed."

He got into bed beside me. He turned on his side and stared at me, his hard features soft as he looked at me. He'd shaved his beard yesterday, so now the beautiful skin of his chin was visible. His chest rose and fell as he breathed, and he stared at me just the way he used to.

Like he'd found peace.

"This bed is only comfortable when you're in it. Trust me..."

I turned and cuddled into his side. I pressed my face close to his, his cologne wrapping around me. I was assaulted by the smell of his body soap and his cologne. He smelled exactly the way I remembered.

New York seemed like a distant memory now.

"What's on the agenda for tomorrow?" I whispered.

"I have no plans."

"Based on what you told me, you need to get back to work."

His eyes combed over my features, taking me in with his intense gaze. "I don't care about that right now. All I care about is you." He hooked my leg over his hip and kissed me, bringing me against his hard-on in his boxers.

Just as we used to do every night before bed, our hands were all over each other. Our mouths moved together passionately, and we tugged on each other to get closer. He gently ground against me, his cock rubbing against my throbbing clit.

His hand fisted my hair as he rolled on top of me, kissing me like he never had before. It was slow but more intense. He felt my lips like he was discovering them for the first time. His embraces were gentle, but when he fisted the back of my thong and dragged it down my legs, he wasn't gentle at all.

I wasn't even sure why I'd worn it to bed since he was going to rip it off anyway.

He pushed his boxers past his ass and then situated himself on top of me. With one quick thrust, he pushed himself inside me, sliding through my wetness until he was balls deep. His lips paused against mine as he breathed through the pleasure, his dick soaking wet from my arousal.

I locked my ankles around his waist, securing him to me so he couldn't slip away ever again.

He kept his cock buried inside me as he looked me in the eye. "We're going to see how much come you can take tonight."

"Good." My nails dragged down his back. "I've always wanted to know."

WHEN I WOKE UP THE NEXT MORNING, CONWAY was gone.

I opened the nightstand, looking for my phone Conway had replaced for me, and that's when I saw the magazines and the bottle of lotion. The pages that were dog-eared had images of me, photos that Andrew captured of me.

There were several.

I guess he wasn't kidding.

When he told me he hadn't been with anyone else, I believed him. But seeing the evidence right in front of me was both touching and arousing. Instead of picking up another beautiful woman, he chose to pretend I was still there.

Why did it take him so long to come get me?

I put everything back in the drawer then looked out the window over the terrace. Despite the storm that had happened the night before, it was a sunny day. The sun wasn't as bright and it had a hint of fall, but it was still beautiful.

I spotted Conway on the terrace, sitting in his swim trunks while he drank his coffee and read the newspaper. He'd obviously had a swim, so he was back to exercising. And the omelet and toast on his plate was a good sign too.

I made my way downstairs, and I encountered Dante in the hallway.

"Sapphire, I'm so glad you're back." It was the nicest thing he'd ever said to me, especially since he usually didn't say anything at all. "Conway asked for a big breakfast with a basket of toast. And he even went for a swim. He's so much better. You make him better." Dante smiled then walked back into the kitchen.

I moved outside to the terrace and saw Conway sitting under the umbrella. The water had dried off his skin, but his hair had flattered and was still a little damp. He looked up from his newspaper when he heard me, and that handsome smile slowly infected his face.

I leaned down and kissed him. "Morning."

"Morning." He cupped my face and rubbed his nose against mine. Rubbing noses was the kind of affection I saw between happy couples, so I guessed that meant we were a happy couple. "How'd you sleep?"

"Like a rock." I sat in the chair across from him, and

when I saw the breakfast laid out in front of me, I released a sigh of happiness. I'd missed mornings like this, when Dante would prepare a fresh omelet and fresh baked bread. Everything was so peaceful here, so slow. There seemed to be an endless amount of time to do anything. In New York, it was about constantly being on the go. There never seemed to be enough time to do everything.

But here, time wasn't an issue at all.

I sipped my coffee and savored the smooth taste. The mug was warm in my fingertips, and the fresh omelet with sun-dried tomatoes was delicious. In New York, I had to cook for myself, and no matter how hard I tried, it never turned out anything like this.

Conway folded his newspaper and set it to the side. He sipped his coffee and stared at me, giving me his undivided attention the way he usually did in the evenings.

"You can keep reading your paper."

"I'd rather look at you."

Instantly, I melted like a piece of chocolate on top of warm dough. I'd dreamed about this man every night for three months. I'd imagined these conversations, these tense expressions. I'd imagined being the center of his world again.

"What are your plans today?" he asked.

I could get to the stables while the weather was still nice or take a last-minute dip in the pool while it was still warm. But there was something much more important that needed to be done. "We need to get to work in the studio, Con."

"You just got back. We can take a few days."

"No." There was nothing I wanted more than to take a ride on the horses to see that view of Verona again. I wanted to spend all my time with Conway, making love under the oak tree or sipping coffee together. But there wasn't time for that. "You've fallen behind, and we're in a serious time crunch now."

The corner of his lip rose in a smile.

"So let's focus on that. When you're done with your line, we'll take the time to do something else."

"Anything in mind?" he asked.

I would love another trip to Greece or somewhere else

beautiful, but just being locked away in his bedroom was enough. "Making love."

"Good answer."

We finished breakfast then moved to the third floor. The table was covered with an assortment of fabrics, and his sketchbook was flipped to a white page with random scribbles on it. He'd made one drawing, scratched it out, and tried to draw another drawing on top of it. One day on top of the other, it showed his inability to stick with one idea. Anytime I saw him press his pencil to the paper in the past, he always sketched a beautiful piece—on his first try.

He dropped his bathing suit bottoms and changed into his sweatpants, but he kept his chest bare. His tan had faded slightly from being indoors all the time, but being exposed to the sun for the last hour had made his skin glow again.

He surveyed the mess on the table, his biceps clenched hard in displeasure. "My mind has been unfocused lately..."

I organized the different pieces of fabrics and hung them up on the organizer. Then I arranged his tools, his pins as well as his special pair of scissors. I put everything back the way he liked because his arrangement had been seared into my memory.

I grabbed a piece of deep blue fabric, silky in texture and soft against my fingertips. "This is pretty."

"It is." He leaned against the table, his sketchbook beside him on the surface.

"How about something with this?"

"I've already used a similar color."

"Alright…" I hung it up on the rack and pulled out a red color.

"No," he said immediately. "Nothing red."

"What's wrong with red?"

"Not your color."

I returned it then looked for a new shade of color, something that might look good against my skin tone.

"The color isn't what matters."

I stopped and turned to him.

"The color accentuates, yes. Picking the wrong color tone can completely upset everything. But when you start from the ground and work your way up, the design and fit are the most important. Nail those, and then worry about that other stuff later."

"Alright...then where should we start? I can tell you which pieces are my favorite. Maybe that can get your inspiration going."

He straightened beside the table, his long frame tightening with strength. His broad shoulders matched his broad chest, but his hips narrowed dramatically at his waist. He was a perfect triangle, a symbol for the ideal physique for a man. But his body couldn't compare to his chiseled face. Like an old-fashioned movie star, he had a distinct hardness to his face. With a beautiful jawline and intense eyes, he belonged in front of the camera rather than behind. "You want to inspire me, Muse?"

It seemed like a trick question, so I didn't say anything. He was suddenly tense, borderline angry.

He stepped away from the table and walked to the gray couch next to the coffee table. He patted the back of it. "Lie down." He kept one hand on the top of the cushion as he waited for me to respond.

He didn't order me around that often anymore, so his request was a novelty. If he wanted to fuck me, he usually just kissed me and guided me to the nearest surface. I hesitated before I moved to the couch and took a seat.

"Lie down," he ordered.

I lay back, my head resting on the armrest. I was in a sundress that I'd pulled on before I left the bedroom to join him for breakfast, so everything below my thighs was bare. My ankles were crossed, and I stayed still until he told me what to do next.

He grabbed his sketchbook and pencil and sat in the armchair on the other side of the coffee table. He crossed his legs and sharpened his pencil, his eyes on me. With every grind of the head of the pencil, the sound filled the room. His eyes remained locked on me until his pencil was at the perfect sharpness.

Then he rested his elbow on the armrest, grasping the pencil. "When you were in New York...did you think of me?"

"Always."

"Did you think about me when your fingers were between your legs?"

Flashbacks of my nights alone in bed came back to me.

My sweaty, writhing body rose in temperature as my fingers circled my clit. Sweat collected on the back of my neck. I pictured Conway on top of me, his muscled mass thrusting into me deep and hard. My legs always shook when I came, saying his name to the shadows in my bedroom. I wasn't sure why it was so difficult to simply answer him. I thought of the magazines I found in his drawer, along with the half empty bottle of lotion. I shouldn't feel any shame for admitting the truth, not when he was guilty of the exact same thing. "Yes." I couldn't hide the redness that filled my cheeks.

"Show me."

I stared at him blankly.

"Show me," he repeated, this time more aggressively.

I'd touched myself before, but it was always in private. I'd felt it was a shameful act, but when no one was around, it didn't seem to matter. But to have Conway watch me when I could just have the real thing made it feel unbearably awkward.

His eyes narrowed even more. "I won't ask again, Muse. You work for me. Don't forget it."

I still felt innately bashful, but the darkness in his eyes

and the authority in his voice made me want to touch myself anyway.

"Pretend I'm not here."

I finally parted my knees and lifted my dress up enough to reveal my thong.

His eyes shifted down.

My hand slid down my stomach until my fingertips slipped underneath my panties. I glided farther down until the soft skin of my fingertips came into contact with my yearning clit. The second I made contact, I took a deep breath.

It felt good.

Conway rested his fingertips against his lips, the pencil still between his fingers. He watched me, his expression hard and full of arousal.

My fingers rubbed my clit in a circular motion, and I went slow, partially trying to restrain myself from making it feel too good. I was still self-conscious about what I was doing, aware of the man watching me.

"I'm not here," he whispered.

I closed my eyes and pictured Conway on top of me, his

hard body suspended over mine. He pressed me into the cushion, his body taking mine as his. He separated my thighs with his knees so he could get all of his cock inside me. He started to thrust deep and hard, making his balls tap against my ass.

I rubbed myself harder.

My other hand moved through my hair, and my lips parted to suck in more air. My hips started to rock like Conway was really moving me. I stopped paying attention to Conway on the armchair and focused on the one moving between my legs. My fantasies with him always focused on the intimacy, the way my body was bent so he could have all of me.

He had to give me all of his dick every time, to make sure I was completely his. I pictured the darkness in his eyes, the way he clenched his jaw to stop himself from coming deep inside me.

My fingers moved harder.

I felt the slickness drip from my cunt. It smeared onto my fingers when I moved harder. My breathing accelerated, and quiet moans escaped my lips. I always came when I pictured him coming, giving me all of his come. "I want your come..."

Conway inhaled a deep breath from the armchair.

Then I came, my pussy convulsing just as my hips jerked. My head rolled back and I moaned, my eyes closed as I pictured his dick twitching inside me with release. The climax wasn't as profound or long as it was when he was really inside me, but it was still incredible.

Now I didn't care that he was staring at me at all.

I expected him to throw his sketchbook aside, drop his pants, and fuck my soaked pussy. Instead, his pencil pressed against the paper, and the sound of scratches filled the air. He worked quickly, his hand moving in exaggerated motions as he constructed the perfect lines.

I slowly came down from my high, the tenderness between my legs gradually fading. My pussy had tightened during my climax, and now it relaxed once more. The moisture pooled between my legs, but I didn't get up to clean myself. I lay absolutely still, making sure I didn't disrupt Conway as he focused on his idea.

Twenty minutes later, he turned the page. His pencil hit the surface, and he started drawing again, moving on to the second idea in a row.

I watched him, staring at the focused expression on his

face. His eyebrows were furrowed with an intense look. Sometimes his fingers rested against his temple as he kept drawing. Once in a while, he glanced up and stared at me on the couch, like he was remembering the scene he'd just witnessed.

I knew he was constructing some of his best designs in that moment. I knew he'd just hit the jackpot in creativity. I knew whatever he created would shock the world once more. Because Conway Barsetti was the best at what he did.

Regardless of the inspiration.

I FELL ASLEEP ON THE COUCH, AND IT WASN'T UNTIL I heard the sewing machine that I woke up.

The table was disorganized all over again, and the sun was long gone because he'd been working for hours.

I wasn't even tired when I lay on the couch, but after that intense explosion between my legs, the exhaustion had crept into my veins and I slipped away.

I sat up and pulled my dress down, realizing how slutty I looked lying there with my legs spread open.

Conway pulled the fabric out of the sewing machine then grabbed his needle and thread. He made the final touches on the piece, placing the buttons and gems in the fabric.

I came around the table and looked at his sketchbook. Now it was thick with seven different drawings. I took my time and examined each one, seeing the moodier theme accompanying his work. There was a sense of loss, a sense of loneliness. Most of the drawings were black or made with other dark colors like deep purple or olive green. But each one was beautiful, full of potent sensuality. "I like them."

Conway was in his own world, so he didn't acknowledge what I said.

I stood there in silence, waiting for him to say something.

But he didn't. His eyes were glued to his hands, and even though I inspired him with my provocativeness, he didn't seem to care.

I wasn't offended. I was just glad he was working, making up for all the lost time. He'd spent three months doing nothing, and now he was motivated once again. His knuckles were clenched in excitement, and his eyes were narrowed with focus. I knew he didn't ignore my words—he just couldn't hear them.

I walked down the hallway toward my bedroom where I came face-to-face with Dante.

"Sapphire, Vanessa is here to see you."

"She is?" I hadn't spoken to her since I left. Her father must have told her I'd returned. She either wanted to yell at me for changing my number and forgetting about her, or she was just happy that I was back.

"Yes. I'll whip up some dinner, and you two can talk in the dining room."

"Thank you, Dante."

Just the way he did with Conway, he gave a slight bow. It was something he didn't do before, always treating me as a guest of Conway's rather than a resident. But now that had changed, judging by the sign of respect he just gave me.

Maybe he liked me, after all. "I'll be there in a second." I made a pit stop to the bedroom and changed my panties, since they were still soaked from my self-induced arousal. I changed my dress too, afraid that I smelled like sex. The last thing I wanted Vanessa to think about was me having sex with her brother.

I made my way downstairs and stepped into the dining room. Vanessa was already there, wearing a long-sleeved red shirt with black skinny jeans. A glass of red wine was in front of her, along with a basket of fresh bread.

She rose to her feet when she saw me, not cracking a smile. Her eyes narrowed, but it wasn't clear if it was from anger.

My eyes drifted to the floor. "I'm sorry...about everything."

She came around the table and wrapped her arms around me. "Don't be sorry. The only one who should be sorry is my brother. He's a fucking dumbass."

I laughed into her shoulder and hugged her back. "My phone didn't work in New York, so I had to get a new one. I wasn't ignoring you on purpose."

"No, I understand. And I'm sure talking to me would have just made it harder on you." She pulled away and looked at me with the same softness her mother expressed sometimes. She radiated maternal warmth and didn't exude a hint of judgment. Vanessa was sassy, but only when someone provoked her. I'd never seen her say a bad thing about anyone unless she was poking fun at her brother.

We sat across from each other, and Dante served dinner, chicken with rice and vegetables.

I hadn't had rice in months. It looked so damn good.

Vanessa poured me a glass of wine before she ripped off a piece of French bread. "I'm trying not to eat too many carbs, but I can't pass up Dante's bread. He's a genius."

"I know."

"I asked him to show me his secret, but he refused. He's lucky Conway won't fire him. Once I'm making money, I'm gonna buy Dante out from under Conway. I'll pay him double what my brother pays him."

"Good luck. He seems pretty loyal."

"People are only loyal until the money is on the table."

I was surprised she didn't immediately question me about the ordeal with Conway. Maybe her father already told her the details, so it seemed pointless to have that discussion. I didn't want to talk about it anyway, so I guess it didn't matter.

"So, how was New York?" she asked. "Was it nice to be home again?"

Not at all. "I was born and raised there, so I know all the nooks and crannies of that place. The people are interesting, and the opportunities are endless. And the food is great too. But honestly, once I came here, this felt like my home. New York felt like a place I'd been to once before, but it was only temporary. Going back didn't feel right. The second we pulled up to the house here...it finally felt like I was home."

Her eyes softened. "It is your home."

"It's good to be back. And obviously, it's good to be with Conway. I've never been so miserable. I've lost my parents and my brother, and the loss still didn't compare to the heartbreak of losing Conway."

"Aww..."

I picked up my fork and took a bite of my chicken, keeping my gaze down in embarrassment.

"I'm glad Conway finally got his shit together. My father told me he wouldn't commit. I don't know why men are like that. They don't want to be with one woman until they realize they'll lose her if they don't straighten out."

She rolled her eyes. "I think a real man loves his woman like a psychopath. If love doesn't make him crazy, then he's not doing it right."

"I think he's just afraid of how it'll affect his work."

"I think he's just a pussy."

I laughed before I could get the food into my mouth. Only Vanessa had the sass to say things like that.

"But I'm glad he manned up. My father and I never talk about my romantic life because it's way too awkward, but he told me I should only be with a man who's man enough to love me with everything he has—and wear his heart on his sleeve. If he doesn't say he loves me in a room crowded with people, then I need to find someone better."

"Your dad is a wise man."

She shrugged. "That's what they say. He tried to talk some sense into Conway a few times. Carter did too. I guess seeing you with someone else was all he needed to get his shit together..."

I didn't want his family to think I actually slept with someone else. I didn't even date anyone. "The tabloids reported that incorrectly. Nox and I were just friends. I told him I wasn't ready to see anyone for a while, so he said he would settle for my friendship in the meantime."

"Really?" she asked. "Because he was hot. Like, hawt."

I chuckled. "He's pretty easy on the eyes."

"So...is he staying in New York?" she asked with hope in her voice.

"He owns a few gyms there and inherited a nice apartment from his parents, so I don't think he's going anywhere."

"Damn."

"But Mr. Right is out there somewhere, Vanessa. Keep looking."

She sighed. "I'll keep looking, but sometimes I worry I'm too picky. My standards are just too high, and no man can reasonably meet those requirements."

"I think it's good you don't settle. There're a lot of jerks out there."

"True. Conway included."

I chuckled. "No...he's alright."

WHEN MIDNIGHT ROLLED AROUND, CONWAY STILL hadn't come to bed.

He was still working hard in his studio.

I wondered if I should grab him and drag him to bed, but if he was in the moment, I shouldn't interrupt him.

But now that I had him back, I didn't want to sleep without him beside me. I wanted his smell wrapped around me, his delectable warmth. His deep breathing was my lullaby, and with him beside me every night, I never felt so safe.

So I lay there in the dark, eyes wide open as I waited for him to join me.

Thirty minutes later, I heard the door in the other room. He shut it quietly behind him, and then his footsteps sounded on the floor. He was barefoot because he hadn't changed since he walked into the studio. He was just in his sweatpants. His black silhouette appeared in the bedroom.

"Had a good session?"

He pushed his sweatpants and boxers off his body,

stripping until he was in nothing but his skin. His expression was hard to see in the darkness, but I imagined he wore an aggressive look. His movements were quick and short, and he yanked the covers back until my legs were revealed.

He suddenly snatched me by the ankle and yanked me to the edge of the bed. Like a kidnapper grabbing his victim while they slept, he dragged me to the edge then pulled off my panties. He didn't bother with my shirt and sank between my legs, getting his dick inside me like he'd been hard up for hours instead of minutes.

He gave one shove, and he was inside me, buried between my legs. "My muse." He rocked into me hard, fucking me like an animal. All his sweet gentleness was gone, and now he was ferocious. He gripped the back of my neck as he pounded into me, fucking me harder than he ever had. "Mine."

My nails latched on to his back, and I buried my face in his neck, letting him do exactly what he wanted. I inspired his pieces, and now he was hard, just thinking about them over the last twelve hours. "Yours."

11

CONWAY

"WHAT DO YOU THINK?"

Nicole stared at the seven different pieces I'd made, her expression impossible to decipher. She always wore the same look, regardless of the occasion. Even when she was in front of the cameras, she didn't crack a smile.

She passed by each mannequin, her fingers resting across her lips.

I didn't care about her personal opinion. But she had a talent for choosing what the audience would love. "They're amazing. I love the switch in mood. Winter is coming. The dark colors are perfect for that. They'll be an amazing hit for Christmas. I think this is a home run.

Not necessarily better than your last line, but different and unique enough. Where did you come up with this?"

Muse. Watching her touch herself painted perfect fantasies in my mind. I imagined many different scenarios, mostly me catching her in the act, watching because she hadn't noticed me. It was every man's fantasy, to walk in on a woman pleasing herself.

And to find out she was thinking of him.

Walls had surrounded my brain, and I couldn't think through the barriers. The depression and misery clouded my ability to think. My sex life was uneventful because I was jerking off to photographs of my ex.

How could I design a decent piece of clothing?

But now all those restraints had been removed.

I could think clearly again.

"You know how, Nicole."

She didn't look at me. "I'm glad she's back. I was getting worried."

"That makes two of us."

"But I'm also concerned you're too dependent on her."

"Makes two of us…again."

Nicole dropped the subject and made notes on her tablet. "I'll get these to production and coordinate with the retailers. They'll want to be as prepared as possible for this line. When did Sapphire return?"

"A few days ago."

Nicole turned to me, her eyebrows hiked nearly off her face. "You did all this in a few days?"

More like twenty-four hours. "Yeah."

"Jesus…she must be some woman."

Oh, she was.

"I'll take care of all this. Did you have a date in mind for the next show?"

"No. Whenever you think is best."

"Alright."

I walked back into my office and found Muse waiting for me. She was flipping through a magazine, her legs bent and pulled toward her body. Her hair was curled that day, and smoky makeup was on her eyes.

"How'd it go?" She set the magazine off to the side.

"Nicole liked everything." I opened a drawer in my desk and pulled out my checkbook. After a quick calculation, I wrote down the amount I owed. "She was shocked I made everything so quickly."

"I'm still shocked about it."

"Well, when inspiration hits you..."

I grabbed the check and walked toward her. "There's something I want to know."

"Yes?" She looked up at me, smiling once her eyes met mine.

I moved into the seat beside her and wrapped my arm around her body. I pulled her close to me, the smell of her hair immediately surrounding me. "What's your last name? You've never told me."

"You've never asked."

I pressed a kiss to her neck. "What is it?"

"Swanson."

"Sapphire Swanson...pretty."

"Thanks."

I grabbed the check and added her last name to the line. "Your first paycheck."

She took it from my hands and eyed the number with disappointment. "I don't think this is right."

"Not high enough?"

"Too high." She handed it back to me. "I'm supposed to pay you back for everything."

"And you are. I'm taking ten million out every month." I handed it back. "So this is yours."

"Oh..." She eyed it again, like she'd never seen a big check before. "But what about my apartment?"

"It's included. By the way, my guy says he put it on the market. He has a lot of interest already."

"Wow, that was fast."

"I think you can get more than what you paid, so you might even make a profit from it."

"I only lived there for three months, so I'd be surprised."

"And the fact that it's already furnished really helps."

"I guess...if people want my old things."

"When the Realtor tells them you used to live there, I'm sure they'll want to keep everything."

She folded the check in half. "So I just go down to a bank and deposit this?"

"Yep."

"Maybe I should buy myself a car."

"Why?" I demanded.

"So I can run errands and do things...live my life. What do you mean, why?"

"I have seven cars in the garage."

"But I don't want to drive one of those. I want something more practical, like an SUV or something."

If I had my way, she wouldn't drive anywhere. If she needed to be somewhere, my guys could escort her there. I wanted her under my surveillance at all times, but I knew that was unrealistic now that she was permanently living with me. She had the same kind of sass like all the other women in my family, so she wouldn't put up with my protection forever. "I can help you pick one out."

"Thanks."

"How about we go to the bank now? I'll give you a ride."

"Yeah, that would be great."

I got out of the chair then straightened my tie.

She stood in front of me then rose on her tiptoes to kiss me. "Thanks for everything, Con."

"You just inspired my best work. You don't need to thank me."

"But I do," she whispered. "You've given me so much, not just money in my pocket. I live in a beautiful house with a beautiful man. I'm living a fairy tale. My Prince Charming is a shade darker than the ones in the stories, but I think darker is better..."

My hands gripped her waist, and I pulled her close to me. "What I've given you is nothing in comparison to what you've given me. And I'll spend my days and nights trying to make up for the stupid things I did."

"It's water under the bridge, Conway. Just make love to me every night, tell me I'm beautiful every morning, and tell me you love me over dinner. That's all I want."

"Then you'll have it."

My parents came over for dinner.

It was the first time we were all together since the shit hit the fan. My dad knew the truth about my relationship with Muse, and that meant my mother knew too. But I knew they would never tell Vanessa.

"We brought a bottle of wine." Dad walked inside with a bottle in hand. "It's from the best harvest we produced this year. Bold and smooth, it'll go with anything Dante is preparing for tonight."

"Thanks." I took the bottle. "I'll tell him to put it on ice."

He patted me on the back then gave me an affectionate look. He didn't hug me the way he usually did, our last few conversations still palpable between us. I'd done a lot of things to disappoint him, and while he still loved me, it wasn't the same as before.

My mom came in next, and like nothing had happened at all, she embraced me on the doorstep. She hugged me tightly, like she was still the mother of a young boy. Her hands gripped me with motherly affection. "Hey, Con. You look good."

"Thanks, Mom." I kissed her on each cheek before I pulled away. "And you look nice, like always."

Vanessa came next, giving me a glare instead of a hug. "Con."

I rolled my eyes. "Vanessa."

We moved into the dining room, where my parents greeted Muse with a hug. They talked to her for a bit before they allowed Vanessa a moment to say hello. My sister and Muse hugged, and then Dante poured the wine.

We gathered around the table and sat down, immediately breaking into the bread and butter.

I sat beside Muse, aware of how awkward this gathering was. Muse had been gone for three months, and everyone knew it was because of me. I'd thrown this beautiful woman away and forced her to return to New York and move on without me.

They all judged me for it.

But no more than I did.

My father started the conversation. "Are you happy to be back?"

"Very," Muse said. "I was born and raised in New York, but Italy is my home. This place is my home..." Her eyes shifted to me for a moment. "And it's nice to see you guys again. You've always been so nice to me, made me feel welcome."

"Because you're a sweetheart," my mother said affectionately. "And any woman who can get my son to straighten up is wonderful in my opinion."

Muse smiled then tore off another piece of bread.

Vanessa kept up her glare. "Don't fuck it up again, alright?"

My father snapped his head in her direction. "Vanessa." He only used her name, but that was enough to get her to settle down.

Vanessa dropped her glare and avoided his gaze by drinking her wine.

My sister annoyed the shit out of me, but her heart was always in a good place. "She's right. And don't worry, Vanessa. I won't."

She raised her glass to me. "I'll drink to that."

Muse couldn't hide the smirk on her face.

We dug into our meal, and like the last three months had never happened, the conversation started to feel normal. Vanessa talked about school, my mom mentioned the winery, and they asked Muse what she would be doing while living here.

"I'll still be helping Conway with his business," she said. "He just submitted a new line of designs to his assistant. He's trying to push the release right before the holidays."

"That's great, Con," Mom said. "I'm glad to hear you're back at work."

Only because my inspiration had returned. I couldn't count the number of times I'd stared at that sketchbook without a single thought in my head. When I jerked off to her pictures, I wasn't inspired by that either. She was wearing another man's lingerie, pieces I didn't respect, so that didn't unleash my creativity either.

Only when she was back in my arms and under my roof did I put my pencil to the paper. I let the emotions and hormones guide my hand, and I constructed something that was vaguely apparent in my mind.

"Will you be doing any modeling?" my father asked.

"No." I spoke before Muse had a chance to answer.

After seeing sensual pictures of her online and in magazines, I was determined to hide her from the public eye. As long as she was my woman, the only time she would be photographed was when my arm was wrapped around her waist.

My father gave me a look of amusement. "No surprise there."

"I enjoy helping with the horses," Muse said. "But now that winter is coming, I'll need to find something else to do. I would try cooking, but Dante is very particular about who he allows in his kitchen."

"Why don't you just do nothing?" Vanessa asked. "It's what most women do when they're with a rich dude."

"Because I'll get bored," Muse said with a chuckle. "I can only work out so many hours a day. After that, I need to do something else. Working in the stables is nice because there's always something to do with the horses. But once winter comes, Marco won't need me anymore."

"Maybe you should take some classes," Vanessa said. "Learn Italian."

"Yeah," Muse said. "That's a—"

"She's not taking any classes," I interrupted. "If she

wants to learn Italian, she has me."

Vanessa took a long drink of her wine, showing her obvious irritation for me.

Just like when I was a boy, I wanted to rip off a piece of bread and throw it across the table and hit her in the face. "Father, how's the winery?" There was always something new going on at the family business, so that should get them talking for a while.

"Good," my father said. "Uncle Cane and I are considering expanding a little more."

Muse moved her leg under the table and gently rubbed it against mine, showing the smallest affection in private. She kept her eyes on her food and pretended she wasn't doing anything at all, and the believable performance was even more endearing.

I liked feeling her touch me, even when my family was around. She wanted me at all times, even after the fierce way I broke her heart. My hand moved to hers on the table, and I took it a step further by placing my palm on top of hers.

She turned to me, a slight smile on her lips.

I squeezed her hand in return.

12

SAPPHIRE

CONWAY FOLDED ME UNDERNEATH HIM, MY LEGS bent and open to him. My hips were turned at a deep angle, and I was pinned against the mattress and unable to move. I looked up at the handsome man on top of me, observing the intensity in his eyes and the tightness of his jaw. He slowly rocked into me, giving me his large length with gentleness like he'd never given it to me before.

My hands moved up his arms, and I gripped his muscles as I breathed with the motion. Quiet moans escaped my lips with every single movement, feeling him stretch me over and over. He didn't fuck me hard like he had the other night. Now this was slow, so slow.

Instead of kissing me, he preferred to watch me. He

watched my chest rise with the breaths I took, watch my lips part when a moan erupted from my throat. He studied the way my eyes changed when I felt the head of his cock hit me all the way inside.

A guttural moan escaped his lips sometimes, a masculine sound that made my spine shiver from the top of my neck to the bottom of my ass. His weight pressed me into the mattress and pinned me down in a locked position. His hard body rubbed against mine as we moved together, his strong chest dragging against my hard nipples.

The sex was slow but packed with powerful intensity. I could feel the ache between my legs, feel the desperation for a deep combustion. I teetered on the edge of the oblivion, prepared to slip away at any moment.

He kissed the corner of my mouth, his breath coming out shaky. "I love you." He spoke against my mouth, his hips thrusting so he could fit every inch of his cock inside me as he said it. "So damn much."

I gripped his shoulders and felt my pussy tighten in reaction, loving the sound of his deep admission. He told me he loved me before, but not like that. He didn't put his heart on display and lay everything bare. He said it like a confession, words that he meant from the bottom of his heart.

Before I could say it back, I came all around his dick. I squeezed him tight, cut into him with my nails, and slipped into a sensual orgasm that made me writhe, whimper, and moan all at the same time. "Con...I love you too." My come slathered his dick, sheathing him in such a pool of moisture that he was completely soaked in it.

"My woman..." He pressed his hips deep between my legs, getting every inch of his dick inside my pussy before he released with a moan. With his balls against my ass, and his face far above mine, he came. His voice was masculine in nature and full of satisfaction.

I moaned again even though I was finished, loving the way he enjoyed giving me every drop of his come. I loved feeling it sit inside me, loved feeling it drip from between my legs because there was so much of it.

When he finished, he pressed a kiss to my forehead and pulled out his softening dick. A web of my moisture stuck to the crown of his cock and my entrance, stretching before it finally broke apart. A drop of come was still on the head of his cock.

He got off me then grabbed the clothes he was wearing that day, a navy blue suit and a black tie. He was heading off to work while I stayed home for the afternoon. He usually cuddled into my side after sex, but he needed to get to work.

That was fine by me. Now I got to go back to sleep.

He pulled on his clothes, adjusted his cuff links, and straightened his tie. He leaned over me on the bed and kissed me on the forehead. "That come better still be there when I get back."

"Of course."

It rained that afternoon, so I was stuck inside. While the house was big, there wasn't a lot to do except work out in the private gym. I hated working out on a machine, and now that I wasn't a model anymore, I couldn't find the motivation to pick up the weights again.

So I decided to organize my stuff in his room. I hadn't really unpacked my things because I'd spent most of my time being naked. I hung up my clothes in the closet and sectioned off my wardrobe by occasion. My finer dresses went into a different section, and my everyday wear was pushed to the front. Conway didn't mind making room for all my things, but his walk-in closet would allow it.

When I organized my stuff in the bathroom, placing my makeup bag in the drawer and my hair products in the cabinet, I came across a box of tampons. Conway had thrown some of my used toiletries away, so these were either new, or he bought them when I returned.

But when I looked at them, I realized I hadn't had my period yet.

According to my calculations, I should have started three days ago.

The terror gripped my heart, but it quickly faded away when I realized how absurd I was being. Three days wasn't enough to cause a panic, and that shot I took was still good for a while longer.

I had nothing to worry about.

CONWAY CAME HOME LATER THAT NIGHT, LATER than usual.

"Long day?"

"You could say that." He pulled off his tie and dropped it on the ground. The rest of his clothes were placed in piles on the floor, breadcrumbs throughout the bedroom.

His clothes were too expensive and important to leave on the ground, so I trailed behind him and picked them up. I put them on a hanger to be dry-cleaned once Dante collected the laundry after dinner.

"What are you doing?" he asked when he was just in his boxers.

"You shouldn't leave your clothes on the ground."

"They're dirty."

"I highly doubt they are, and even if that's true, they don't belong on the ground. They'll get wrinkled."

"That's why they're being dry-cleaned."

I shot him a glare.

He smiled in return. "Alright...I'll hang them up next time."

I placed everything on the hanger by the door so Dante could fetch it later. "So, how was the studio?"

"Well, Lacey Lockwood decided to take off."

"Take off in what way?" I asked.

"She decided to join Lady Lingerie with Andrew."

"Oh…" I didn't see that coming. "I'm surprised."

"He took a dig at me." Conway ran his fingers through his hair. While this was a stressful situation, he spoke like it was nothing to be concerned about. "He knows I won't use you as a model, so he took my top performer. He overpaid for her and he knows it, but he doesn't care about losing the money in this situation. Putting me out makes it worth it." He lay back on the bed, sexy in just his black boxers. He pulled the front of his shorts down and revealed his long cock. Then he patted his stomach, silently commanding me to get on top of him.

"That's how you ask for sex now?" I asked with a laugh.

"I'm not asking," he said seriously.

I removed my shirt and panties then straddled his hips. I pointed his crown at my entrance then slid him inside, feeling his thick cock stretch me right away.

He gripped my ass cheeks. "My come still in here?"

"Yeah…pretty sure."

He dug his fingers into my ass. "Good." He guided me up and down his length, his eyes locked on mine.

I held myself up, arched my back, and sheathed his cock over and over. I worked up a sweat immediately since I was doing all the work. He lay there and enjoyed me, aroused by the sight of me working so hard to take him. "What are you going to do now?"

He palmed one of my tits in his hand. "I don't know."

I pushed him deeper inside me, feeling his old come and my arousal sheathe him down to the balls. My movements slowed every time I felt the wave of pleasure wash over me. "I have an idea…"

"Unless it involves your mouth around my cock, save it for later." He guided me up and down aggressively, making me take his cock deeper and harder.

"What if I model for you this time?" I asked through heavy breaths. "Lacey was your best model and—"

"No." He gripped the back of my neck, seizing control. "Now shut up and fuck me."

I listened to his command and took his dick over and over. His hand loosened on the back of my neck, and he moaned with my movements, the sound erupting from him. "Like that, Muse..."

I watched the arousal deepen in his gaze, watched the way his jaw tightened as I rode his dick the way he liked. His look of enjoyment and the feeling of his cock inside me put me on the brink of pleasure. Rubbing my clit against his hard body pushed me over the edge. I fucked his dick harder as I came, my hips convulsing and my pussy tightening. I covered his dick with my come and felt the air escape my lungs. "Conway..." I loved saying his name when I came, loved worshiping this man for everything he made me feel.

He closed his eyes for a brief moment as he let his body slide into oblivion. He pulled me tight against his body as he came, pumping more come into my already full pussy. "Muse..." He released a groan from deep in the back of his throat, a sound full of satisfaction.

He palmed both of my tits when he was finished then placed his hands underneath his head. He lay there with tired satisfaction, happy to keep his dick inside me as he softened. He never looked as sexy as he did when he came, all of his masculine instincts escaping.

I ran my hands up his chest, massaging his hard body as I

felt his cock soften inside me. "I still think I should model for you."

"No." He yanked me toward him then pressed a kiss to my mouth. It was soft, his eyes open as he looked at me. "You already have a job, Muse. You're the mastermind behind all my creations. You're the desire, the fantasy that's stitched into every piece of lingerie. I'm sharing my inspiration with the world—but I'm not sharing you."

"But you don't have enough time to replace her with someone else."

"I've got lots of girls, Muse."

"But not like her. She takes the lead for a reason. I don't want Andrew to hurt you. He's taking a shot at you because he knows you won't use me. So fire back by using me, by making headlines with my comeback...this one time."

His eyes shifted back and forth as he looked at me.

"It's the perfect idea, Con. No one will care about Lacey when they see I'm working with you again. We'll have an incredible show and get people talking about it. No one will even care about Andrew." I felt like this was my fault. If I hadn't gone to Andrew, this wouldn't have happened in the first place.

He considered it for a long time before he gave an answer. "I'll think about it. That's the best answer you're going to get from me right now."

Conway stood with Nicole in the aisle between the seats in the auditorium. They were preparing for the show, having the girls run through the motions in the lingerie he designed. A new girl had been promoted to headline the show, but even I didn't think she had what it took.

She was a beautiful girl, of course. But something wasn't working.

I stood beside Conway and listened to him and Nicole talk.

Conway had his arms crossed over his chest and his fingertips resting against his lips. "The formation is correct, the music is good...but something isn't right. It's not standing out against the other shows. Perhaps we should change the theme."

"We can't change the theme," Nicole said. "Not when it has to be centered around the holidays."

Conway had been working on this all week, and I could tell he was stressed by the tightness in his jaw. It wasn't sexy like the way he clenched it in bed. This expression was packed with uncertainty.

"My suggestion still stands..."

Conway and Nicole both looked at me.

"What suggestion?" Nicole asked, her gaze turning to Conway.

I let Conway answer, that way he could decide what he wanted her to know.

Conway went with the truth. "Sapphire thinks she should headline the show. It'll get people to focus on us instead of Lacey and Andrew."

"That's not a bad idea," Nicole said. "Actually, it's a great idea. I think we should do it, Conway."

Conway looked at the stage where the models were working with the choreographer. He released a deep sigh.

I knew what that sound meant.

He dropped his arms to his sides. "We'll do it this one time. But that's it. After that, she's permanently removed from the lineup. We'll have to spend the next few months finding the next woman to be the face of Barsetti Lingerie—because it won't be Sapphire."

CONWAY DROVE BACK TO THE HOUSE IN THE RED Ferrari he had temporarily loaned me. One hand was on the wheel while the other rested on my thigh. When we drove through the countryside, he didn't need to shift the gears because we were driving straight for a long time.

"Thanks for putting me in the show. I won't let you down."

He released a sigh that was barely audible. "I hate the idea of people looking at you, but I'll admit, it's the best option right now. It'll make everyone forget about Lacey and Andrew. Plus, the designs are beautiful."

"I agree. I don't want anyone to talk about them. I only want people to focus on you."

He didn't smile, but affection entered his eyes. "I appreciate that."

"You're the best for a reason—and I want it to stay that way."

"With a model like you, it'll stay that way." He patted my thigh.

I looked out the window, seeing the sun disappear over the horizon. It was getting darker much earlier now. And it was colder too. I had to wear jeans and a jacket before we left the house.

"The show is on the twentieth, so we have some work to do. It'll be a busy week."

My eyes snapped open when I heard the date.

It was already the twentieth?

That meant I was thirteen days late.

Thirteen.

Shit.

My heart slammed in my chest, and sweat formed at my temples. Anxiety kicked in as the fear crushed my lungs. When my period was late at first, I just brushed it off. But two weeks was way too long.

That could only mean one thing.

The hormone shot was ninety-nine percent effective.

So how did this happen?

I'd only been living with Conway for three weeks. He managed to get me pregnant that fast, even on birth control? We were making love several times a day, but that wasn't unusual for us.

Fuck.

WE SAT ACROSS FROM EACH OTHER AT DINNER, eating salmon steaks with broccoli and carrots. I was back to my model diet, only eating high protein with no carbs. Dante uncorked a bottle of wine, but I didn't have a glass—blaming it on the calories and sugar.

I had to get a pregnancy test. That was the only way to confirm the truth.

But how would I get one?

Conway didn't like it when I went anywhere alone, and now that I was with him all the time, there was no way for me to sneak off.

I only had one option.

Conway watched me from across the table. "Everything alright, Muse?"

"Yeah...just tired." I pushed the carrots around then took a bite of the broccoli. I had been hungry all afternoon, but the second I suspected I was pregnant, I completely lost my appetite.

What if I was pregnant? What would Conway think?

Would he be angry? He said marriage and kids were on the table, but he wasn't ready to make that kind of commitment. If I were pregnant, it would completely change the relationship. He might not even want me in the show anymore.

So I had to find my answer. And if it was what I feared, I had to come clean about it.

Conway took a bite of his fish, still watching me. "You seem distracted."

"I'm just thinking about those heels I'll have to wear. It's been a while since I hit the runway like that. When I did photos with Andrew, I was almost always barefoot."

Conway drank his wine, his veined forearms looking muscular in his t-shirt. "You'll be fine, Muse. You're the best model I've ever seen—you're a natural."

I forced a smile, still feeling the acid that built up in my stomach. "Thanks..."

We finished dinner, and before Conway downed the rest of his wine, his phone rang. He glanced at the screen. "It's Carter. I've got to take this." He stepped out of the room and pressed his phone to his ear. "What's up?"

The second he was gone, my smile turned into a frown and I slouched at the table. My anxiety rocked my chest at full force. I only had a few minutes before he returned, and then I would have to pretend everything was normal.

When nothing was normal.

I needed a pregnancy test, so I'd have to come clean about it if I wanted to get one. But I didn't want to bother Conway with this unless I absolutely had to. If the test was positive, I would have to decide what to do then.

But if it was negative, there was no point in turning his world upside down.

Dante walked inside, his black apron still secured around his waist. "Are you two finished?"

"Yes..." My chin was propped on my knuckles, and I was hardly aware that he was there.

"Everything alright, Sapphire?" Dante had never inquired about my personal well-being before, but ever since I'd returned to the villa, he treated me with the same respect and care as Conway.

"Uh..." I wasn't going to dump my problems on the chef, but then an idea came to mind. "There's something I need you to do for me...and you can't tell Conway."

He stiffened at the comment, clearly uncomfortable by the suggestion. "You know I'm loyal to Mr. Barsetti. I don't get paid to keep secrets from him."

"It's not really a secret. I just need something, and I can't ask him to get it for me."

Dante stacked the dishes in his hands. "What is it?"

"A pregnancy test..."

He took a deep breath, his expression narrowing. "I see..."

"If I'm not pregnant, I don't want to worry him. But if I am..." I never finished the sentence because I wasn't sure what I was going to say anyway. The stress was making my chest crack right down the middle. Everything ached. The only reason I didn't want to be pregnant was because I didn't want Conway to be disappointed. I wanted him to want our baby...not be upset about it.

"I understand, Sapphire. I'll get it for you."

"Thank you."

"I'll get it after I do the dishes and collect your laundry. I'll leave it in the cabinet where the coffee mugs are in the kitchen. You can grab it when you're ready." He stacked the rest of the plates in his arms and walked out.

This was really happening. I was really going to take a pregnancy test.

And I felt terrible for wanting it to be positive. I didn't want to trap Conway into a commitment he didn't want. I didn't want him to be stuck supporting me forever. But if I were going to start a family, I would want it to be with him.

I wanted to start a family with him.

CONWAY ALWAYS SEEMED TO WANT TO BE ON TOP.

Every night before bed, he moved between my legs and kissed me at the same time, making love to me instead of aggressively fucking me the way he used to.

I never asked for it, but I would gladly take it.

But tonight, I wasn't feeling it. I kept thinking about that pregnancy test waiting for me downstairs. When he went to sleep, I would slip away and finally get the answer that had been gnawing at my side constantly.

I needed to know.

Conway must have noticed I wasn't as wet as I usually was, and my kiss wasn't as deep as it used to be. He shoved himself completely inside me, broke our kiss, and then stared at me. Everything came to a halt, and I could feel the tension before he even said anything. "What is it, Muse?"

"Nothing." My hands glided up his back.

Concern faded away, and annoyance entered his gaze. "When I'm buried to the hilt inside you, I can feel everything you feel. So tell me."

When I was the recipient of that gaze, I almost fessed up. I wanted to share the burden with him so I didn't have to carry the stress on my own. But I still couldn't tell him the truth, not when I didn't have the answer first. "I guess I'm just a little sore. We've been making love a lot lately."

He studied my gaze for another moment, as if he was trying to figure out if I was lying. But then the softness returned to his gaze. "Do you want me to stop?"

"No..." My mind wasn't in the moment, but it still felt good. "I want you inside me." I pulled his face to mine and kissed him, distracting his mind by getting him to focus on our embrace.

His hips started to move again, and he thrust into me, my legs pinned back toward my waist. He moved deep and slow, breathing with me in the darkness of his bedroom. A minute after that, it was like the conversation had never happened at all.

I WAITED UNTIL HE'D BEEN ASLEEP FOR AN HOUR before I made my way downstairs and opened the cabinet where Dante hid the pregnancy test. I found the small box concealed behind the coffee mugs and then made my way back upstairs to the third floor.

In the middle of the night, the house was dead quiet. All the lights were off, and Dante was asleep in his private quarters on the bottom floor. The second floor wasn't even used because the place was so big.

I returned to our bedroom and spotted Conway still sound asleep in bed. He was turned on his side, his arm still in front of him as if it were wrapped around my waist. I went into the bathroom and locked the door behind me before I examined the box.

I'd never used a pregnancy test before, so I read the directions with shaky hands before I opened it. Fortunately, there were two sticks inside, so if I messed up, I had another shot. I sat on the toilet and did my business before I placed the stick on the counter.

Then I waited.

I was supposed to wait two minutes before my results appeared, so I sat on the lid in my panties and t-shirt and waited.

I waited a damn eternity.

Whenever life got tough, I always tried to put things in perspective. Nothing was ever as bad as it seemed. There was nothing I couldn't overcome. A psychopath had chased me all the way to Italy, and I was kidnapped by the Skull Kings. At that point, I thought I was going to be raped and murdered.

So being pregnant, even if Conway was upset, didn't seem that bad.

He might flip out the way he had when I told the world I loved him. He might get furious and push me away. But after he calmed down, he would come back to me. We would figure out what to do.

But I was jumping ahead because I still didn't know the results.

Two minutes passed.

But I still didn't look.

"Oh god…" I pulled my knees to my chest and rested my chin on my legs. I was afraid to look at the results because I already knew what it was going to say.

I could feel it in my gut.

I finally grabbed the stick and read the word written on the window of the strip.

Pregnant.

13

CONWAY

Muse picked at her egg whites but didn't take more than a few bites. Her French bread beside her was smeared with Dante's homemade jelly, but she only took a single bite, probably trying to eliminate the carbs. Her eyes were downcast for the entire meal.

"I'm going to have you end with the black one-piece I created. I know it should be centered toward a holiday theme, but people don't love Christmas lingerie that much. Nicole says you should wear a Santa hat, but I'm not going to do that. I think I'm going to have you wear red pumps, though. That subtle touch should be enough."

She moved her omelet around, her shoulders hunched forward and her face as pale as milk. Her makeup was done for the day, but even the cosmetics couldn't make her features stand out. They were washed out and unremarkable.

"Muse?"

"Hmm?" She jerked slightly and looked up, obviously having no idea what I just said.

She'd been out of it since yesterday. When we made love before bed, her mind wasn't connected to me the way it usually was. While she didn't seem angry with me, she was definitely distant.

Was she starting to regret taking me back?

Did she miss Nox?

Did this feel like a big mistake to her?

Or was I just being paranoid, letting my own insecurities get to me? "I said I was going to have you wear red heels, despite the fact that Nicole wants me to push for more of a Christmas theme."

"Oh...that should be nice." She looked down at her food again, but she still didn't eat anything.

"Are you sure there's nothing wrong?"

Her head popped up, and her eyes widened as the guilty expression came into her face. "No...I just didn't sleep well."

I didn't want to accuse her of lying, but something told me she wasn't being completely truthful. "What is it? If you don't want to do the show, you don't have to."

"No, that's not it..."

"Then what is it?" I pressed.

She pursed her lips together tightly, her eyes avoiding mine. "It's nothing...we should get going. We have a long day at work." She set her napkin down and excused herself from the table.

"You barely touched your food."

"Yeah...I just don't have much of an appetite today."

MUSE DID THE CHOREOGRAPHY WITH THE OTHER girls, getting down the technique and formations of the show. She looked exemplary in the different designs that I made, probably because they were custom-made for her body.

The other model I originally had was boring in comparison.

As much as I didn't want Muse to be visible to the public eye, she'd already been gawked at in photographs for the last three months. Young men already had her pinups on their walls. One more show wasn't going to make much of a difference.

Nicole stood beside me, watching the choreographer work with the girls. They ran through the show with the music several times, but a lot of progress needed to be made. Fortunately, they had two weeks to get it down.

Nicole turned to me. "Everything alright with Sapphire?"

I guess I wasn't the only one that noticed. "Why?"

"She can't seem to concentrate today."

"She's been that way for a few days. Every time I ask her what's wrong, she makes an excuse."

"Well, you need to drag it out of her soon. We can't have a model this distracted."

The show was the least of my concerns right now. I was more terrified that Muse's happiness had something to do with me. Maybe she wanted more from me, and I wasn't giving it to her. I told her I loved her almost every single day, and I'd given in to her demands.

What more did she want from me?

The drive home was spent in silence.

Muse looked out the window while she fidgeted with her fingertips in her lap. Like she was purposely trying to avoid my eyes, she kept her gaze glued out the window. The awkwardness made it seem like we were strangers instead of lovers.

I was tired of the bullshit. "Muse, I'm not going to ask you again." I kept my gaze on the road, my knuckles turning white from gripping the steering wheel so hard. "Even Nicole noticed you were distracted. I've been patient, but my patience has officially worn out. So tell me, or I'll make you tell me."

"Make me tell you?" she whispered.

"You bet your ass I will. Now tell me what it is, or I'll drag it out of you."

She pressed her forehead to the window and closed her eyes.

Jesus Christ. "Goddammit, Muse. Tell me. Are you okay? Please tell me you're alright." I'd never seen her act this way before. She always spoke her mind, even when I didn't want to hear what she had to say.

"Yes, I'm okay," she whispered. "I just need a little more time."

"A little more time?" I asked incredulously. "You've shut me out for three days."

"Conway—"

"Do you regret taking me back? Do you want to go back to New York?"

"Of course not."

"Then what?" I took a breath of relief, but I was still pissed.

She turned quiet again.

We pulled into the roundabout at the house, and I handed the car over to the valet. We walked inside the house, and her continued silence only pissed me off more.

"Muse, why won't you tell me? It's me."

She kept walking. "Just give me a little more—"

I grabbed her by the elbow and yanked her back toward me. "I love you. You love me. What the fuck is it that you can't tell me? I treat you like a goddamn queen. I kiss the ground you walk on. But you're refusing to share your life with me, and I think that's a bunch of bullshit."

She twisted out of my grasp then walked toward the stairs, shutting down the conversation with her silence.

No matter how hard I pushed, she resisted. She said she was okay and she wasn't leaving me, so what was so difficult to talk about? How could she not trust me? How could she not confide in me? I watched her walk to the top floor and disappear down the hallway.

Maybe it was best she walked away. My anger was making my nostrils flare, and I couldn't see straight. I'd never been very patient, but when it came to my woman keeping a secret from me, I was even less patient. I'd asked her about it three times, and she still refused to open up to me.

"Hello, sir." Dante stepped into the hallway and took my coat.

I ignored him, my eyes still on the stairs where I'd last seen her. I moved my arms so he could get the coat off me, but I was barely aware that he was there.

"I don't mean to intrude..." He lowered his voice to a whisper, even though Muse was so far away she couldn't overhear us anyway. "But be a little more patient with her, Conway. She's just scared right now. Comfort her and make her feel safe...and she'll open up."

My eyes flashed to his face, the suspicion entering my gaze. "You know?"

"No...but I have a hunch."

"Why don't you just tell me, Dante? You work for me, not her."

He folded my jacket then draped it over his arm. "Trust me, it would be much better coming from her instead of me."

BEFORE I STEPPED INSIDE OUR BEDROOM, I DROPPED my insufferable attitude and tried to adopt a new demeanor. Sometimes I was suffocating because I needed to be in control of everything. I knew how overwhelming I could be. She was the object of my fascination, so naturally, I was obsessed with every thought that came across her mind.

I stepped inside and found her sitting on the couch. She was still in the same clothes she'd been wearing, and her legs were crossed, as well as her arms. The TV was off, so she sat in silence, her thoughts her only entertainment.

I stripped off my tie and draped my suit jacket over the back of the chair at the desk. I was tempted to pour myself a scotch to calm my nerves, but alcohol didn't seem appropriate in that moment.

I came around the couch and sat beside her, doing my best not to stare at her so openly. My hand moved to her thigh, and she didn't flinch at my touch. "Muse, I didn't mean to come off so aggressively. You're my whole world, and I'm just worried. I want you to know there's nothing you could say to me—to change us. There's nothing you could do to change my love for you." She could even tell me that she'd slept with Nox, and it still wouldn't change where we stood. I loved this woman more than I could ever fathom, and there was no way I was ever letting her go again. Maybe this was forever, but the idea of a lifetime didn't scare me—not when it came to Muse. "Whatever you're keeping inside is obviously bothering you. It's killing you. Tell me what the problem is, and we can get through it together." I squeezed her thigh.

She was unresponsive, staring at the coffee table.

My jaw clenched and I wanted to start screaming again, but I took Dante's advice and remained calm, understanding that quiet confidence was preferable to hostility. My fingers moved gently over her thigh, touching her lightly. I stared at the blank TV screen and waited.

And waited.

Finally, Muse took a deep breath. "I've been scared to tell you because...I'm not sure how you're going to react."

"I'll tell you how I'm going to react, Muse. I'm going to be right here—no matter what you say."

"You say that now..."

I kept massaging her, doing my best to be calm. "You have to tell me anyway, Muse. You may as well get it over with. All I know is, I love you. No matter what comes our way, we'll make it work. I didn't treat you right in the beginning, but the last three months has taught me how terrifying my life is without you. I don't want to feel that way again..."

She gave a slight nod.

Maybe we were making progress.

She lowered her arms, and in one of her hands was a plastic rod. She placed it on my knee then pulled away.

It took me a second to figure out what it was. I'd never seen one in the flesh. I raised it toward my face, seeing the word written in blue.

Pregnant.

It took me another few seconds to absorb what I'd just read.

Pregnant.

Muse was pregnant.

There was a baby growing inside her at this very minute.

I leaned forward and held the pregnancy test in both hands, staring at the blue letters with even more attention. I needed more time to process this, to understand that my world had changed in an instant.

She'd only been with me for two weeks, but I knew I was

the father. I didn't need to ask if she'd lied about Nox because she wouldn't do that to me. Muse was always honest with me.

I was going to be a father.

I was going to have a son or a daughter.

A little Barsetti.

Jesus Christ. It hit me then. My world had completely changed, had flipped upside down. In a few months, I would be responsible for another person. I would worry about them just the way my parents worried about me. Until the day I died, this child would be the biggest thing inside my heart.

I nearly forgot Muse was still sitting beside me, watching every single reaction.

"I don't know how it happened," she whispered. "You gave me that shot when I first got here, and I know it lasts twelve months. I didn't mean for this to happen, and I want you to know that you're the father. I was never with—"

"Shh..." I set the pregnancy stick on the table and grabbed her hand. I pivoted my body toward her and looked at the terror in her eyes. She was on the verge of tears, afraid of how I would react. When she first told me she loved me, I threw her out of the house and told her to leave.

I didn't blame her for being so worried.

It was my fault.

I brought her hand to my mouth and kissed all of her knuckles. "Muse, it's alright."

"You aren't mad?" she whispered.

"Mad? No, not at all. And I know I'm the father. There was never a doubt about that."

"I just...I know you said you weren't ready for marriage and kids. I don't want you to think I did this on purpose, that I'm trying to trap you."

"I don't think that at all, Muse." My hand moved into her hair, and I cupped her cheek. I tried to erase the fear in her eyes by enveloping her in my confidence. "No, I'm not ready for marriage and kids. I wanted more time for it to be just us. But it was going to happen anyway. I was never going to let you go, so if you ever demanded I put a ring on your finger, I would do it...because I can't live without you. This baby doesn't change anything. It doesn't make me love you less. It makes me love you more." I pressed my forehead to hers. "I want you to relax now. I promise I'll always take care of both of you. I will be the best father I can be, and I will be the best husband I can be."

"I'm not asking you to marry me, Con. Just because—"

"I do want to marry you." I tilted her head, forcing her to look up at me. "I want us to be a family. I want both of you to have my last name. I'm never going to feel this way about another woman as long as I live."

She finally smiled, the fear slowly dissipating from her eyes.

"It's sooner than I wanted, yes. But it doesn't mean I don't want it." My hands moved to her flat stomach. There was no sign of life, not even a small bump. But just knowing a piece of her and me was deep inside was enough for me.

"Con...there's always the possibility that the baby won't make it to full term. So maybe we should wait..."

The sentence offended me, deeply. I'd barely accepted the fact that I was going to be a father, and now I was already attached to the idea of us being a family. I was already scared of losing the life growing inside her.

"Don't talk like that." My hands rested against her belly, protecting her from everything. "I want to spend my life with you no matter what—because I love you."

AFTER A LONG SESSION OF LOVEMAKING, MUSE passed out under the sheets. The long nights of stress had caught up with her, and now that she knew everything would be alright, she finally got some rest.

I went into my office. It was nine in the evening, and I'd skipped dinner. Dante seemed to understand we didn't want to be bothered that evening. I opened a brand-new bottle of scotch, poured a glass, and thought about everything that had happened in the past few hours.

Shit, I was gonna be a father.

No, I wasn't expecting it.

And fuck no, I was not ready for it.

But my fear wouldn't change the future, so I needed to accept what was to come and man up.

When Muse was so afraid of what my reaction would be, that forced me to be strong for her. It forced me to be the rock that she needed me to be. She already had all the stress on her shoulders because the baby was living inside her.

My job was to make her calm.

Mission accomplished.

But now, it was my time to freak out.

When I grabbed the phone, I debated who to call first. Carter was my best friend, but for some reason, that didn't feel right. The only person I really wanted to call was my own father. When my mother was pregnant with me, he said he wasn't ready to start a family. But the accident ended up being the best thing that ever happened to him.

So I called him.

Despite the late hour, he answered almost immediately. "Con, are you alright?" Protective and serious, he was ready for the worst possible news. He'd lived a life of crime before I came along, and old habits died hard.

"Yeah, I'm alright. But I need to talk to you...in private."

"Give me a second." He turned to speak to my mother in the background. "I've got to take care of some business,

Button." The sound was then muffled as he walked to his office in a different area of the house. Once the door clicked behind him, he spoke again. "I'm here."

"Well...I'm not sure how to say this. I guess I'm just going to say it."

"Alright." He turned quiet, letting me have the floor.

"Sapphire is pregnant." I said the words out loud, and once I heard them, they felt even more real. She was having my baby. I would be a father. We would be a family. Just yesterday, all I cared about was my lingerie show. Now that seemed so damn insignificant.

My father was quiet for a while. "I wasn't expecting you to say that, son."

"I wasn't expecting her to say it to me either."

"I hate to ask...but is it yours?"

"No doubt." I wasn't going to get a test done. If Muse said she didn't sleep with anyone else, I believed her. Just as she believed that I hadn't been with anyone else either. There was no reason for either of us to lie. Even when we were apart, we were committed to each other... because we loved each other.

My father didn't press that topic any further. "How do you feel about it?"

"Kids were the last thing on my mind..." I knew I could be honest with my father. He wouldn't judge me for anything I said.

"That was how I felt when your mother was pregnant with you."

"I'm not ready for any of this, but that doesn't matter. Sapphire was really scared to tell me. She was afraid of my reaction, not that I blame her. But seeing her so scared made me want to make everything better. So I told her it would be alright, that it would be okay."

"It will be okay, Con. Once the shock wears off, it'll get easier. Every man is afraid to be a father. Every man is afraid he won't do a good job. Any man who thinks fatherhood is easy and simple obviously hasn't put much thought into it."

"Yeah..."

"Did you offer to marry her?"

My dad would punch me if I didn't. "Of course."

"And did she say yes?"

"Not formally. She said we didn't need to get married if that's not what I wanted."

"She doesn't strike me as a woman who would try to trap you. She seems like she genuinely loves you...for who you are."

"She does." I had no doubt of that. "Which is why I want to marry her. I've never felt this way about another woman before her. When she told me she was pregnant, it made me think of what you said to me...that just because I wasn't ready didn't mean it wasn't already happening. Maybe I wasn't ready to love her...but I do love her. Maybe I'm not ready to be a father...but we're a family. And maybe I'm not ready to be a husband, but I've already committed my whole life to her."

"Exactly."

"I don't want another woman as long as I live."

"So this is a blessing."

"It is," I whispered.

"Congratulations. I'm very happy for you. It's hard to see now, but having children is the greatest joy you'll ever know. When they're young...when they're old. It's like having your heart live outside your body. I didn't think I'd love anyone more than your mother...and then you were born. Then Vanessa was born...and your mother moved to the bottom of the list. It's strange...hard to understand until you experience it yourself. Right now, this seems like the most stressful day of your life. But when you look back on it, you'll realize it's the happiest."

"You're always right, Father. So I believe you."

"And I'll always be here if you need advice."

"Yeah," I said. "I'm lucky that I have you as a father. Most people don't have what I have, so I can ask the best of the best. Makes it a little easier." I didn't realize what I'd said because it tumbled out of my mouth so quickly. I was speaking from the heart, unfiltered.

My father didn't say anything for a solid minute. He just sat on the phone, letting the silence stretch between us. "One day, your son or daughter is going to say something like that to you...and you'll know it was all worth it."

I TOOK THE DAY OFF FROM WORK BECAUSE THE SHOW didn't seem important to me anymore.

Nicole was both pissed and confused. It was unlike me to drop the ball like this.

But I didn't care what she thought.

I lay beside Muse in bed while I waited for her to wake up. She must be catching up on sleep because she should have been awake a while ago. But she kept sleeping, hooked into my side like a child holding a teddy bear.

When she finally woke up, my face was the first thing she saw. "Con..."

My fingers moved through her hair, and I placed a kiss on her forehead. "Morning."

She stretched beside me before she buried her face in my neck. She hugged me as she woke up slowly, her arm squeezing my waist.

My fingers drifted down her back, feeling the smooth skin.

She took her time waking up, her breathing slowly increasing until she was finally awake. Then she pulled away and propped herself on one elbow. "What time is it...?"

"Nine-thirty."

"Shit, really?" She squinted at the clock on my nightstand to make sure I was right. "We've got to get to work." She scooted herself to the edge of the bed.

"Whoa, come back here." I grabbed her by the elbow and gently tugged her back toward me. "We aren't going to work today."

"You want me to stay home?"

I pulled her back into my side and placed a kiss at her hairline. "We're both staying home today."

"But why?" she whispered.

My hand moved to her flat stomach. "I don't want to work today. I want to spend time with you." My fingers felt her tiny belly button and the small abs underneath her skin.

"I know you have a lot of work to do for the show…"

"I don't give a shit about the show," I said seriously. "I'm staying here—with you."

Her eyes softened in a way they never had before. "That's so sweet…"

"I thought we would try to make breakfast together."

"In Dante's kitchen?" she asked in surprise.

"Yep."

"And you think he'll be okay with that?"

"I told him to take the day off."

"Do you know anything about cooking?" she asked.

"Nope."

"This should be fun," she said with a laugh.

"You can teach me. And then we can eat what's edible before we order a pizza."

"I've never seen you order a pizza before."

"I used to before I could afford a guy like Dante."

"I can't even picture that." She rubbed her hand up my chest, in a much better mood than she was last night. Now, she couldn't stop smiling. She couldn't stop looking at me like she was a very happy woman.

"Looks like you're about to see for yourself."

"Have more faith in yourself than that. I'm sure you can make some breakfast. But I admit...I would love to see

Dante's reaction when he opened the door to a pizza delivery person."

"Me too."

MUSE AND I MADE A MESS IN THE KITCHEN AS WE prepared pancakes, eggs, and bacon. I burned the first batch of eggs, so I had to make a second one. Muse took care of everything else since she was a lot faster than me.

We left a tornado of dishes behind.

Dante wouldn't be too happy.

We stood at the counter as we ate, pancake batter on our clothes and spots of grease on our skin.

"Pretty good," Muse said.

"Just as good as the stuff you made me in New York."

"Maybe we should cook more often."

I glanced at the dishes and shook my head. "No thanks."

She chuckled. "It's not so bad. The dishwasher does most of the work." She dragged the pancake through the syrup then popped it into her mouth. It was the most I'd seen her eat in days, and now I was glad her appetite had returned. "I feel like I owe you an apology."

"Me?" I asked. "Why?"

"I should have told you sooner. I shouldn't have assumed—"

"Don't apologize." I set my fork down and inched closer to her, my face almost touching hers. "You had every right to be afraid. And it makes me very happy that you aren't afraid anymore."

"Well...you took the news a lot better than I thought you would."

I kissed her forehead, smelling the syrup on her lips. "I'm a very happy man. I'm successful, rich, and now I have a woman who's giving me a family—a legacy. To be anything but happy would be an insult to all those people who have nothing. And I certainly don't have nothing."

14

VANESSA

I FINISHED MY PAINTING AND LEFT IT ON DISPLAY IN the hall to be judged by the other students. I didn't consider myself a great artist, but I was good enough to convey a story. I sketched out the details of the faces before I added the paint and brought it to life. The image I decided to depict now was my parents working together in the vineyards. Husband and wife, they were a team as they created a living directly from the soil. It depicted Italian culture, Italian pastimes.

Maybe it was stupid to spend money to go to university to pursue a hobby. Becoming a professional painter seemed very unlikely, and if I didn't believe in myself, why should anyone believe in me? But I didn't have any other interests. I didn't want to work in a restaurant, and

I didn't want to go into business like everyone else in my family.

I craved a simple life.

More than likely, I would take over Barsetti Vineyards. But right now, my family didn't need me. Might as well spend my time exploring my other talents. Besides, I loved living in Milan. It was nothing like Tuscany, but it was a great experience. This time away from my family taught me to appreciate them more.

I left campus and walked to my apartment in the center of town. I lived alone because my parents didn't want me to have roommates. My father paid my rent and gave me an allowance to spend every month. When I first came to Milan, taking his money didn't seem strange. But now that I'd been living there for a year, I'd started to hate it.

I didn't want his money anymore.

That motivated me to make my paintings good enough to sell. If I could make enough money just to cover my expenses, I wouldn't have to rely on my father's support.

And I knew that would make him proud.

I walked up to my door and shoved the key inside. But the lock was already undone.

Did I forget to lock it?

It wouldn't be my first time, so I stepped inside.

My apartment wasn't big, just a one-bedroom with a small living room and a tiny kitchen. As a single person, it was all I needed.

The second I stepped inside, I noticed something was wrong.

All the lights were off. I always left a few on so I wouldn't have to step into the darkness once the sun was gone. My eyes fell to the large shape sitting on the couch, the outline of a man's shadow. I didn't need to see his face to know he was hard like steel. And I didn't need to ask why he was there to figure it out. "You know, breaking and entering is against the law." As a Barsetti, I refused to cower in fear. I'd hold my head high, regardless of the way my life would be taken from me. I was a very proud woman. "And you picked the wrong apartment to rob. I'm a poor-ass college student. I don't have shit to take." I flicked on the light beside me, illuminating the living room and kitchen.

The man sitting on the couch was big and ugly. He wore a cold sneer, and his eyes were lit with amusement. His hands were empty of a gun or a knife, but that didn't downplay his dangerous vibe. Dressed in all black with a scar along his eye, he was the stuff of nightmares. Anyone else would scream their head off.

I didn't, but that didn't mean I wasn't scared.

He released a cold chuckle. "You're either very stupid or very brave."

I set my bag on the floor, making it thud against the tile from the weight of the books. "You have to be a little stupid in order to be brave. And you're forgetting proud. You came in here thinking you could catch me off-balance. You don't know who you're dealing with." I stepped into the kitchen and turned my back to him. I opened the fridge, pretending everything was casual. Anyone else would grab a kitchen knife, but I seemed to be looking for a snack.

Little did he know, I kept my biggest steak knife right on the top shelf.

He rose from the couch and sauntered toward me, an amused expression still on his face. "You really are your father's daughter—arrogant."

"You want something to eat or what?" I grabbed the knife and kept it hidden behind the door.

"There's no one out here looking after you, little girl. So you can drop the tough girl—"

I shut the door and stabbed the knife right into his chest.

His reflexes were astonishingly fast, so he pivoted his body just in time to protect his heart. The blade went into his shoulder, halfway in. He groaned then snatched my wrist and flung me hard onto the ground. "Dumb fucking bitch." He yanked the knife out and tossed it on the counter, the metal clattering with the sound and spilling blood everywhere.

I hit my head on the floor, but I didn't let the disorientation slow me down. I climbed to my feet and reached for the glass cookie jar so I could slam it on his head.

"Nope." He grabbed me by the ankle and dragged me toward him across the floor. "I had no intention of hurting you. But now, you've pissed me off." He pulled his hand back and slapped me hard across the face.

I turned with the hit but refused to show any sign of

pain. "You picked the wrong family to fuck with, asshole."

He kneeled down on top of me, staring at me with his disgusting expression. "No. Your brother shouldn't have crossed me."

"And who are you?" I spat on his face. "A real man doesn't go after the weakest prey. He fights a man his own size."

"But you aren't the weakest, sweetheart." His hand moved to my face, cupping my cheek. "I find you very fascinating."

I turned my face and bit down hard on his thumb.

He yanked his hand away and slapped me again. "Calm down, bitch. If your brother cooperates, you're home free."

"What do you want from him? Money? Who are you?"

"Money?" he asked with a laugh. "No, I don't give a damn about money. But he took someone that belongs to me...a woman that should be mine. He has to give her back...or I'll keep you instead."

The only woman I could possibly think of was Sapphire. "Sapphire?"

"Yep."

My brother loved her and would never give her up. And she was my friend...so I didn't want her to hand herself over anyway.

That meant I had to get out of this on my own.

But how?

15

CONWAY

I WALKED INTO THE BEDROOM AND DROPPED MY jacket on the ground. Like every other day, I stripped off each piece of clothing and didn't give a damn where they fell. But once I saw them on the ground, I realized Muse would pick them up.

And I didn't want her doing anything.

I gathered my clothes again and hung them up so Dante could take them after dinner.

Muse stepped out of the bedroom and into the living room, dressed in a dark blue dress that reached past her knees. She was only a few weeks pregnant, so there was no visible change in her body. But to me, she was already glowing.

"How was work?" she asked.

"Everything is coming together." My body was starting to return to normal now that I was exercising every day. When it was too cold to swim, I went to the gym and lifted weights. My abs were thicker, and my biceps were stronger. "Nicole thinks you should still be in the show."

"In a few weeks, I'll be a month along. It might not be obvious, but I'll still be a little bigger than I should."

"Even if you are showing, I think that's fine. It'd be sexier anyway."

"Sexy?" she asked. "Men don't fantasize about pregnant women."

In the past, I would have said the same, but now that my woman was pregnant, there was something innately sexy about it. Knowing I was the one who knocked her up gave me a new sense of purpose. "I don't agree with that. I think any man who has a pregnant wife is turned on every time he looks at her."

"I don't look pregnant yet, so you don't know."

I looked her up and down. "Oh, I know."

She moved into my body and wrapped her arms around my neck. "So, what are we going to do?"

"It's up to you. Do you still want to do it? Because you don't have to if you don't want to."

She tilted her head back to look at me, her eyes lit up as she stared into my face. "Yes, I want to."

"Are you sure?"

"Yes."

I rubbed my nose against hers before I kissed her on the forehead. "Then I'm going to make an announcement that we're having a baby together. I think that will attract even more attention to the lingerie."

"Are you sure that's a good idea?" she asked. "Maybe we should wait—"

"Don't even talk like that." I silenced her with my tone. I didn't want to entertain my thoughts with the horrible possibility that she could lose our baby. A week ago, I didn't want children, but now that she was pregnant, I would do anything to protect that baby growing inside her.

She rested her forehead against my chin. "Alright. Then let's do it."

"Perfect." I rested my lips against her forehead. "I made an appointment with a doctor in Milan. He's the best in Italy. We'll see him tomorrow."

"Oh, that's great. Thank you."

"I'm sure he'll want you to take some prenatal vitamins or something." My fingers moved underneath the fall of her hair.

"Did you tell Nicole?"

"Yeah."

"What did she say?"

"Congratulations. Stuff like that."

"Have you told anyone else?"

"I called my father the other night."

"Really?" She stepped back to look up at me. "What did he say?"

"He's excited. It's his first grandchild."

She rested her face against my chest. "I'm glad he's

happy about it. I wasn't sure how your family would feel about it."

"What are you talking about?" I wrapped my arms around her. "They adore you."

"I just don't want them to think I did this on purpose…"

"They don't. My dad told me to settle down with you many times. When you were in New York, he came by the house and tried to talk me into it. So don't worry about what they think of you. You make me happy, and that's all they care about." I rested my chin on her head and held her in my arms. She was so tiny in comparison to my large stature. It made me want to protect her even more, to protect the life that we made together. "I'm sorry I ever let you go…"

She tightened her arms around my waist. "Let's forget it, Con. I'm here now…we're together. That's all that matters."

I squeezed her a little harder, feeling the guilt crush me. "You always believed I loved you, even when I said I didn't."

"I saw it in the way you looked at me…just the way I see it now. I know you better than you know yourself."

"Yes." I closed my eyes. "Yes, you do." I held her for minutes, treasuring the feeling of her small body against mine. Whenever I came home and looked at her, there was usually one thing on my mind. But right now, I just wanted to hold her. I treasured this woman so deeply. I loved her more than I'd ever loved anyone else. She'd become my whole world, and now I couldn't believe I'd ever let her go.

My phone started to ring in my pocket. I was going to ignore it because I didn't care at that moment, but Muse pulled away.

"You should get that." Her hands trailed down my stomach as she stepped away. "I'll still be here when you're done." She gave me a slight smile before she walked away and headed into the bedroom.

I fished out my phone and saw the number on the screen, a number I didn't recognize. I took the call and held the phone to my ear. "Conway."

A heated voice came over the line, a tone I'd recognize anywhere. I'd only been exposed to him twice, but you never forgot your enemy's presence. "Barsetti, how's it going?"

It was Knuckles. I didn't need to ask to make sure. "I

would ask what you want, but I don't care." I was glad Muse walked into the other room. I didn't want her to hear any of this conversation. I didn't want her to feel scared, not when she should only be concerned about the baby growing inside her.

"Don't call my bluff, Barsetti. Not when I have something you want."

"You don't have anything I want."

"Don't be too sure of that," he said with a chuckle. He turned away from the phone and spoke to someone in the background. "Vanessa, say something to your brother."

"Go. Fuck. Yourself." Vanessa's deep and powerful voice rang over the line, carrying the pride of the Barsetti line. She must have been kidnapped and trapped, but she still held her head high. I didn't need to check to make sure it was her. It definitely was.

Knuckles came back to the phone. "Looks like I do have something you want—"

"Touch her, and I'll fucking kill you." The cords in my neck almost burst open, and spit flew from my mouth. I was so calm just a second ago, holding my woman in my arms, and now I was filled with enough adrenaline to break down a concrete wall with just my hands.

"Give me what I want, and no one gets hurt," he said calmly. "I hate to admit it...I actually respect your little sister. She's got quite a fight in her..."

I didn't care about money, not when it came to my sister. I'd sell this house in a heartbeat to get her back. My sister and I bickered back and forth a lot, but at the end of the day, I'd lay down my life for hers. I loved her so damn much. "How much, Knuckles? How much do you want?"

"It's not about how much," he said. "Money comes and goes. I want something invaluable, priceless."

I already knew what it was before he even said it.

"I want the priceless jewel that you call Sapphire. Let's trade."

"You can't break the Skull King oath." I bought Muse fair and square at the Underground. According to the rules, he couldn't take her. It was punishable by death.

"And I'm not. I'm not breaking in to your house and dragging her out by the hair. I'm offering you a deal. If you want Vanessa Barsetti, you have to give me

Sapphire. If you don't want the deal, fine. I'll make use of Vanessa instead."

I clenched my fists so hard my knuckles almost tore out of my skin.

"What's it going to be?"

I was silenced by the gravity of the situation. If it were anyone else, I would make the trade. My sister was my family. Nothing was more important than family. But Muse was carrying my baby. She had a little Barsetti inside of her. There was no right answer. And I didn't want to make the trade because I couldn't afford to lose either of them.

I loved them both.

He chuckled into the phone. "It's a difficult decision. I'll give you a few hours to decide. Just remember, whoever I get will be raped and tortured until I get bored with her. So you need to decide who you love more...your sister or your whore."

I LEFT THE BEDROOM AND STORMED INTO MY OFFICE

without saying a word to Muse. I only had five minutes before she figured out something was wrong.

I had to make those minutes count.

Depending on when Knuckles captured Vanessa, he could still be in Milan.

There was a good chance he was.

Vanessa still had a fiery attitude, so she couldn't have been captive for long. Like all prisoners, her spirit would eventually break down. The fact that she still talked back was a good sign.

She wasn't taken that long ago.

So yes, he was still in Milan.

This was entirely my fault, so I wanted to shield my family and not get them involved. I didn't want to worry my parents, to make them terrified of losing their only daughter. But I knew this situation was too important for my arrogance.

I made the hardest phone call I'd ever had to make.

My father answered, in a good mood. "I hope you don't mind, but I told your mother about the baby. You have no idea how happy she is."

I couldn't bask in my mother's happiness, not when I'd never been this scared in my life. All the joy I'd just given my parents was about to be yanked away. "Father…I need you and Uncle Cane to get on a plane here as quickly as possible. I don't know how to say this, but since I don't have much time, I've just got to blurt it out. Vanessa has been taken by an American crime lord named Knuckles. He's been obsessed with Sapphire for the last year, and now he wants to make a trade. Sapphire for Vanessa. He's given me a few hours to decide."

Instead of screaming into the phone or asking a bunch of questions, my father remained calm. He remained so fucking calm that I couldn't wrap my mind around it. "Do you have any idea where he is?"

"Milan."

"You're certain of that?"

"He took Vanessa not too long ago."

"How do you know that?"

"Because she's still being a smartass in the background."

Still calm as ever. "I'll be there in forty-five minutes with backup. Take Carter with you into Milan. Bring guns."

"Alright."

"Do not make that trade, Con."

I was shocked he said that. "Don't?"

"No."

"But Vanessa…"

"Sapphire is family now. We'll get them both back."

I didn't know much about my father's past, but listening to him speak with such confidence gave me a small sense of calmness. "Alright. I'll head to Milan with Carter. I'll try to put a tracer on the phone to figure out where he is."

"You can try, but it won't work. You said Vanessa was in the background?"

"Yes." How could he talk about my kidnapped sister without skipping a beat? I definitely wouldn't tell him the last thing Knuckles said to me.

"How close was she?"

"I don't know…I could hear her pretty well. Why?"

"Grab your security team and take them with you. Next time he calls, listen to her. I told her what to do if this ever happened. She should give us a clue. What did she say when you heard her in the background?"

"She told Knuckles to fuck himself."

"Alright. That means she's in transit. She doesn't know where she is."

"So I should still head to Milan?"

"Yes. I've got to go, Con."

We were both running out of time. I blurted the first thing that came to mind. "I'm sorry...I'm sorry about all this."

"I'm gonna get your sister back. And that's a promise."

"Con, what's going on?" Muse followed me to the front door.

I was carrying two semiautomatic rifles with a pistol on each hip. I was strapped with enough ammo for a war. "Knuckles called me. He has Vanessa, and if I don't trade you for her...he's going to kill her."

Muse halted and covered her mouth with both hands.

Tears sprung to her eyes immediately, her reaction quicker than anything I'd ever seen. "No…"

"My father is meeting me in Milan. Carter and I are leaving now. We think she's still there."

"Do you know where she is?"

"No. But we'll figure it out." Once Vanessa was safe, I'd put a bullet in each of his eyes. He'd tortured Muse long enough, and now he was going to pay the ultimate sacrifice for laying a hand on my sister. He'd unleashed the ferocity of the Barsetti family.

"Con, just trade me," she begged. "Please."

I turned back around, shooting her an incredulous look.

"Please," she repeated. "Vanessa doesn't deserve this. She did nothing wrong. This is all my fault…he wants me. If anything happens to her—"

"I'm not trading you."

"Con—"

"I'll get her back."

Tears poured from her eyes down her cheeks. "I couldn't live with myself if something happened to her."

"Neither can I. Which is why I'm going to get her back." I grabbed the back of Muse's head and pressed a kiss to her lips. It was hard and quick, conveying the affection I wished I had more time to show her. I didn't know what was going to happen. I might die in the fight. Maybe I wouldn't make it back, and I would never meet the little person living inside her. "If I don't come back, you'll be taken care of."

"Don't talk like that…"

I pressed my forehead to hers and closed my eyes. "I'll do everything I can to come back. But I'll also do everything I can to save my sister. My family will take care of you."

"I don't need anyone to take care of us," she whispered through her tears. "We just need you to love us."

I pressed a kiss to her forehead. "I will. No matter what happens, I always will." I couldn't bear the sadness on her face any longer, so I turned around and walked out the front door. Carter was there with his men, and my men were ready to go too. I got into the passenger seat of one of the SUVs, while Carter got behind the wheel.

Carter drove off, ignoring the speed limit and sprinting down the country road.

I didn't look back to see if Muse was watching us.

I couldn't bear to watch her cry anymore.

Carter drove with one hand on the steering wheel, some of his crew sitting behind us in the second row. "Anything new?"

I stared out the window, feeling utterly helpless. I had to sit still for thirty minutes when my heart was racing inside my chest. There was so much adrenaline, so much anxiety. "No."

"Are you sure he's in Milan? That's exactly where we'll guess he is. This guy can't be that stupid."

"Milan is a big place. Besides, there's nowhere else to go. It's just the countryside once you're past it."

"I would just hate to come all the way out here and be wrong."

"Trust me, Carter. I would too…"

"We've gotta put this guy down for good. His whole crew too. No survivors."

"Agreed." I knew how to handle a weapon, but I'd never killed anyone. But that didn't mean I would hesitate to pull the trigger. The second I laid eyes on

Knuckles, he was dead. There would be no surrender.

"As much as you may want to torture him, let it go."

Torture wouldn't give me as much satisfaction as seeing his dead body on the ground. I'd probably throw it in a dumpster where it could be fed upon by rats and other critters from the gutters.

That was more than what he deserved.

WE ARRIVED IN MILAN AND PARKED IN THE GARAGE at the bottom of my building. It was private property, making it easy to hide. The cops would turn the other way if they saw us, but having two cars with armed men would still turn a lot of heads.

My father called me.

"Hey, we're in Milan."

My father responded. "We're about ten minutes out. Where do you want to meet?"

I didn't ask how he got there so quickly. "Garage of my building."

"Alright," he answered. "Has he called?"

Just then, the phone started to beep with the other line. I glanced at it and recognized the number. "He's calling me now."

"Connect it. I'll listen."

I turned it into a conference call. "You said you would give me a few hours." It'd been less than one.

"Changed my mind." I had no idea how he looked on the other line, but his arrogance made me think he was smiling. "What's it going to be?"

"Is she alright?" I demanded.

"Tip-top shape."

"How do I know you're not lying?"

"If she's dead, I have nothing to barter with. And you know how much I want Sapphire's pussy."

I almost slammed my fist into the dashboard. Carter looked at me from the passenger seat, knowing that was going to set me off. But my sister's life was on the line, so the insult wasn't important in comparison. "I need some reassurance first."

"Does that mean you want to make the trade?" he asked hopefully. "Poor Sapphire...guess you never really loved her."

"Prove Vanessa is alive, and I'll answer."

He growled over the line, then there was a pause. He seemed to be moving around somewhere. His voice returned, and he spoke directly to my sister. "Your brother wants to make sure you're alive. And remember what we talked about..." He was warning her not to give away her position.

And I didn't want to know what the punishment was.

Vanessa's strong voice sounded from the background. "Con, kill this fat lady and—"

"Enough." Knuckles walked away, her voice fading into the background as he kept moving. "There. You heard it with your own ears. Your sister is alive and well...for now. Hand Sapphire over, and your sister is yours. Vanessa is a very pretty woman...she might be prettier than your girl. But you know I've wanted Sapphire longer."

I hated knowing my father had to listen to this. "How do we make the trade?"

"We meet in the countryside. You can bring your boys, and I'll bring mine. If we cross each other, none of us will get out of this alive."

I didn't know what else to do but agree to the terms. If I said no, I might not get a hold of him again. Vanessa didn't give any helpful information, so we were stuck. "Let's meet at two. There shouldn't be anyone out at that time."

"Sounds good to me. Wait for further instruction." Click.

Now it was just my father and me. "I agreed because I didn't know what else to do. If we have no idea where he is, we have no choice but to meet him."

"You did the right thing."

Now my heart was beating faster, the terror getting to me. What if I didn't find Vanessa?

"Fat lady..." My father spoke under his breath, talking to himself more than to me.

"What?"

"She told us to kill the fat lady...it's a strange insult."

He was right. I'd never heard her say anything like that in my life. "You're right."

"Hold on." My father took a break from the phone as he considered her words more carefully.

Carter had been listening to the entire conversation. "The only thing I can think of is until the fat lady sings... and fat ladies—"

"Are opera singers." I turned back to the phone. "The opera house. La Scala."

"You're right, Con," my father said in agreement. "It's one of the biggest landmarks in this city. It's unmistakable. Vanessa must have seen it before they pulled her inside."

"There're a few restaurants around the area," I said. "But also a few apartment complexes."

"At least we have an area now," my father said. "Let's meet there, one block over."

"Alright." I watched Carter start the engine. "We'll meet you there."

"Con."

"Yeah?" I said.

"I know you've got beef with this guy, but he's mine. Do you understand?"

I wanted to kill Knuckles for everything he'd done to the woman who was now mine. He'd stalked her, terrorized her. I wanted the assurance that he would never harm her again by putting two bullets in his brain. But I understood that my father's only daughter had been taken, and despite how calmly he spoke, he was furious. His bloodlust couldn't be satisfied until he slit the man's throat. "Yes, I understand."

16

VANESSA

I was placed in a bedroom inside the apartment. When Knuckles transferred me, he put a blindfold over my eyes. But I knew this city like the back of my hand, and every time we turned, I knew what street we were on.

When I turned my face slightly, I managed to get a peek of La Scala out of the corner of my eyes. I was exactly where I thought we were, and then the car drove into an underground garage of a building.

As my father taught me a long time ago, I was supposed to identify my surroundings and convey them in code. When my father told me all this initially, I brushed it off and called him paranoid.

Guess he wasn't so paranoid, after all.

The man who had me didn't seem that interested in me. He only wanted Sapphire, which worked in my favor. But his henchmen were creeps. Constantly touching my thigh in the back seat of the car or smelling my neck, they were totally repulsive.

When my brother was on the phone, I gave them the one bit of information I had at my disposal. I played it off as an insult, and I hoped my family was able to figure out what I was saying.

My life depended on it.

Now I sat on the small twin bed with my back against the wall. The room had nothing in it, like it only existed to house prisoners like me. I had a small window that overlooked the fire escape, but there were bars placed over it.

I didn't see any way out.

My father promised me he would always come get me if this ever happened, but my mother taught me something else. She told me I should never wait to be rescued. The only person I could really rely on was myself. I had to find a way out—at any cost.

Now I was trying to plan an exit strategy.

Knuckles had two men with him, both armed with pistols. He seemed like the kind of thug that had a lot of men at his disposal, but perhaps kidnapping me seemed like such an amateur plan he didn't need more than two men.

I could take down two men.

I would just have to do it one at a time.

I went to the door and knocked. "Hey, assholes!"

Footsteps sounded before the door opened. One of the lackeys stared at me, his gun in his holster and the annoyance in his eyes. He obviously didn't care about his babysitting gig, but his eyes roamed over my body without any shame. "What?"

"What do you mean, what?" I placed both hands on my hips. "I'm locked in this room without water. Even a dog gets a water bowl."

"And you sound like a dog..."

I let the insult slide because I had bigger fish to fry. "Get me a glass of water."

"Please."

"Now," I pressed, crossing my arms over my chest. I turned around and shut the door in his face.

He sighed from the other side of the wood then walked away.

I was trying to get under his skin, trying to anger him so he wouldn't think logically. Then I would be able to make my move when he was distracted.

He returned a moment later with the water.

"Took you long enough." I took the glass then kicked the door shut with my foot.

He sighed again, this time louder.

I DRANK THE ENTIRE GLASS AND WAITED AN appropriate amount of time before I made my move. Just when I stood up to knock on the door, the lock turned and Knuckles presented himself. A beefy man with a malicious gaze, he was terrifying.

I did my best to pretend he wasn't.

"Good, you're here." I tossed the cup at him. "More water." I was the victim in this situation, but I had to exert my power as much as possible. I had to remind him I was a human being, not a punching bag.

He caught it with one hand, his lip curling into a smile. "Your brother has agreed to make the trade. Looks like you're going home." He approached the bed and took a seat, his eyes examining my neck. "If I hadn't wanted Sapphire for so long, I would just keep you instead. We'd be in the Cayman Islands by now, and I'd be breaking you in."

I forced my body not to shiver in disgust. I'd rather die than let this man get on top of me. I'd even slit my own throat if I had to. I was relieved I would be free soon, but I was repulsed that my friend would take my place. I didn't want her to be his victim, to be subjected to the torture he had in mind. "You should keep me. I'm a lot more valuable than she is."

"Yeah?" he asked with interest. "How so?"

"I'm a Barsetti. I come from an honorable family. I'm not the kind of woman who just gives up."

"Sounds like you're giving up to me, by taking her place."

"No. That's me still fighting."

His eyes roamed over my body, particularly my legs. "I've seen very few women who have your kind of beauty. The color of your skin...your hair...your curves." He didn't touch me, but the way his eyes roamed over my body was enough to make me feel sick. "But with Sapphire, it's personal."

"What did she do?"

"Her brother stole from me. So taking her is his way of repaying his debt."

"Why don't you just ask him for the money?"

He grinned. "Because I already killed him."

My body turned to ice.

"So I have to make this trade. I'm sure she'll enjoy the Cayman Islands."

"And you think I won't tell Conway where you're taking her?"

"I hope you do," he said. "He'll come to my turf and be outnumbered. I'll kill him and the rest of his family. And then I'll come after you." He winked then walked out of the bedroom.

I told myself not to be scared, that fear would only

shatter my resolve. If I let it get to me, I might lose the strength to try to escape. Right now, running was my only option. If I could get away, I could save both Sapphire and myself in the process.

But that was easier said than done.

I KNOCKED ON THE DOOR.

The same man who gave me the water answered. "What?"

"I've got to take a piss."

He remained in my way. "Then go."

"I'm not peeing my pants. Gross."

"I'm not letting you out of there." He kept one hand on the door, blocking my path with his size. "So pee in that empty cup."

"I don't have a dick like you do."

His eyes moved down. "I'm going to need proof."

I didn't hesitate before I kicked him in the shin.

He groaned then flinched, his torso jerking down as he moved to grab his leg.

This wasn't part of the plan, but I had to take advantage of the opportunity and go for it. I yanked the gun out of his holster, clicked off the safety, and shot him in the head.

It was the first time I'd ever killed anyone.

I didn't have time to think about what just happened. I didn't have time to process the consequences of my actions. I'd shot a gun before, but I'd never aimed at a person. The man collapsed to the floor, dead instantly.

There was no time for regret. I was doing this to save my life—and Sapphire's.

The gunshot was loud and filled the apartment with the sound of an explosion.

I ran to the front room, looking for the exit so I could dart out of there.

"Knuckles, she has a gun!" The second henchman hid behind the couch and pointed his gun at me. He pulled the trigger, but the shot missed me by less than an inch.

Knuckles came from the other way and snatched my

ankle. He yanked me until I tripped and hit the ground.

I kicked as hard as I could, then pointed the gun in his face.

He smacked it out of the way and tugged on my ankle again.

I turned hard, making my foot come loose. Then I kicked him hard in the nose, hearing it crack loudly.

I snatched the gun and sprinted for the door again.

This time, the lackey shot me—and hit me.

The bullet went into my arm, making my body jerk with the momentum. I'd never been shot, and I had no idea how it would feel. The thing that surprised me most was how painless it was. I didn't feel anything. Completely numb, all I felt was the heat from the bullet. I wanted to fall down and lie still, but I had to keep going.

I might die if I didn't.

I made it out the front door and sprinted down the hallway. I had to push my body to the limit, to keep going no matter how much I wanted to stop. A bullet could enter the back of my skull at any moment.

And this could all be over.

OUR SUVS WERE PARKED RIGHT AGAINST THE CURB, looking conspicuous with their blacked-out windows and bulletproof glass. There were at least twenty men with us, half of them with Carter and me and the other half with my father and Uncle Cane.

My father got out of the SUV and walked toward me, his leather jacket over his shoulders. His black t-shirt underneath looked a little puffy, and I knew that was because he was wearing a bulletproof vest underneath. "We should start on foot. Vehicles are more obvious. And if he's inside one of these apartments, we don't want him to notice us until the last minute."

"Do you think he realized what Vanessa said?"

"Hope not. If he did...we won't see him until the meeting tonight. And we'll have to come up with a different plan."

Uncle Cane came up behind him, dressed similarly and with the same pissed-off expression in his eyes. His gun sat on his hip, and he didn't look the least bit happy to see me. He barely greeted Carter.

When my mother emerged from the back of the SUV, I actually had to do a double take. "What's Mom doing here?"

My father didn't look at her over his shoulder. "Let her be."

"This is no place for her," I argued. "How could you let her come along?"

"He tried," Uncle Cane said. "It didn't work."

My father didn't hide his look of disappointment, but he stuck to his guns. "This is her daughter. There was nothing I could do to get her to stay behind. And she's pretty damn good with a gun. She agreed to stay in the rear."

I couldn't believe that my father, the most protective man on the planet, had allowed this to happen. I didn't consider my mother to be weak by any means, but a war zone was no place for her. "We should split into two groups and circle the block in different directions. If one of us uncovers something, we'll radio to you."

"Alright," my father said. "We'll—"

Gunshots fired into the air.

Our heads snapped in different directions, hearing the backfire echo in the streets. Men pulled their guns from their holsters. My mom was the quickest to draw her weapon.

The gunshots could be caused by anyone, but it was too much of a coincidence.

"It's her," my father said. "Let's move."

We sprinted down the road and cut over onto the next block. We all took different routes, preparing to come into contact with the shooters. I reached an apartment complex with Carter first, and the second we turned to the gate, we spotted her.

Vanessa.

She tripped on the concrete as she ran, the gun sliding out of her hand and hitting the ground. Blood soaked her clothes and streaked down her arm. A gunshot wound was in her left arm, and it was obvious her flesh had just been punctured.

Motherfucker.

I sprinted to her, my gun still secured in my hand. "Vanessa!"

A henchman appeared behind her, his gun raised to shoot her in the back.

Before I could aim and fire, the man had been hit in the chest. He collapsed to the concrete, dead before he hit the ground.

My father appeared from the left, a raging look in his eyes. Smoke still blew from the barrel of his gun.

I got to Vanessa first and held her to her feet. "You've been shot."

"Obviously." She hissed through her teeth, blood still spilling everywhere. "Knuckles shot me when I tried to get away."

My father didn't stop to check on Vanessa. "Conway, get her to the hospital. I've got to—" He stopped when he came face-to-face with Knuckles, a long gun pointed directly between his eyes.

"No!" Vanessa tried to squirm out of my grasp.

I held her tighter, my gun at the ready.

Knuckles sneered at my father. "You thought you could cross me?"

"I did." My father didn't raise his hands in the air. With a strong voice and even stronger stance, he didn't show an ounce of fear. "I've got my daughter back, and Sapphire is safe. You could put a bullet in my brain, but it wouldn't make a difference."

Knuckles pressed the gun harder into my father's skull, his irritation bright in his eyes. He held the gun, but my father held all the power. Even if Knuckles pulled that trigger, he would lose the game. It took all the victory out of it. Once he killed my father, he would be captured by the rest of our men. If he hadn't been so arrogant as to underestimate the Barsettis, he wouldn't have been so careless. I knew he was capable of a better plan than this, a man with more resources than us, but his confidence affected his judgment. If he'd taken the time to learn more about my family, he would have realized this wasn't our first rodeo.

Fucking idiot.

My mom appeared from behind Knuckles, a black rope between her hands. With featherlight steps, she came from around the corner then yanked the rope against his throat, just when my father turned out of the way of the gun. With lightning speed, he broke Knuckles's wrist and snatched the gun out of his broken hand.

And my mom choked him harder, pulling so tight on the rope it was about to snap in half. She tugged on the rope and pulled him to the ground, making his body slam on the concrete. She was half his size and weight, but she managed to drag him several feet, making the rope slice into his skin. A gun was on her hip, but instead of giving him a swift death, she decided to make him suffocate.

My father didn't intervene, letting my mother do exactly what she wanted.

"No one. Touches. My." She watched his eyes roll into the back of his head and his body finally give out. "Daughter." With knuckles strained and white, her hands were about to give out. But when his body collapsed and his spirit left him, she still pulled—like desecrating his remains would give her even more satisfaction.

My father approached her slowly. "Button."

Like she didn't hear him, she continued to tug.

He repeated her name again, this time with more force. "Button, he's gone."

She finally dropped the rope. She stared down at him before she spat right on his face.

"Damn," I said under my breath.

Vanessa was watching the scene too, resting most of her weight on me. "I hate to whine but...I think I need to get to a hospital."

I didn't think my mother had it in her to become a ferocious killer. But the second her daughter was in danger, she turned into someone I didn't recognize. She relished the bloodshed the same way a killer did. "Alright, here we go." I scooped Vanessa up into my arms and waved down a taxi, not wanting to wait for Carter to bring the SUV around.

I carried her into the back seat and looked at the driver's terrified expression in the rearview mirror. "Get me to the nearest hospital."

THEY TOOK MY SISTER TO SURGERY RIGHT AWAY, AND we were left to sit in the waiting room. I was covered in blood, so Carter gave me a t-shirt to change into. The waiting room was packed with other families waiting for news about their loved ones.

My mother and father stood alone on the other side of the room, talking quietly to each other. Tears welled up in my mother's eyes over and over again, and my father did his best to make them stop.

Aunt Adelina came a few hours after that, bringing her daughter, Carmen. They hugged Carter and held him for a long time.

I'd been too busy thinking about Vanessa that I hadn't even thought about Muse. I should pick her up and bring her to the hospital to wait with the rest of my family, but I didn't want to leave just in case we got any news. The nurse told us removing the bullet should be a simple process. It didn't have the same risk factors as open-heart surgery or something more invasive.

I picked up the phone and called Muse.

She answered so quickly I didn't actually hear the phone ring. "Con, are you alright?"

"Yeah, Muse. I'm okay."

"Did you get Vanessa?" she asked in a tear-filled voice. "Tell me you got her."

"Yes, we did."

"Thank god," she whispered. "And no one else got hurt?"

"Well...Vanessa was shot. We're at the hospital while she's in surgery."

"No..." The tears began to pour out, not only escaping in her voice.

"We think she's going to be okay. She was shot in the arm. Didn't hit an artery. But we're still waiting on pins and needles."

"I should be there."

"I'd come get you, but I can't leave the hospital. My parents are pretty upset right now..."

"I understand. Can I have Dante drop me off? Would that be okay?"

Dante would do anything I asked, especially under the circumstances. "Yeah, sure."

"Good. I need to be there. Vanessa is my friend. When I first came around, she was so good to me. She was my friend immediately. I didn't even need to do anything to earn her friendship...it was just natural."

"Yeah, I know." My sister made an effort to make Muse feel welcome in my family. Vanessa was a brat most of the time, but when it mattered, she was there for me. She always had my back, just how I had hers.

"I'll get there as soon as I can."

"Alright."

"I love you, Conway," she whispered into the phone. "I can't wait to see you."

I closed my eyes, loving the way her love reached all the way through the phone. I could feel it, just the way I could feel her lips against mine when she kissed me. Her love didn't understand distance, not when it could cross an ocean in a heartbeat. "Me too."

We got off the phone, and then I looked at my parents again.

My father was holding my mother against him, his chin propped on her head. His hand rested under the fall of her hair while his other hand settled on the small of her back. He hid his emotions like a professional, keeping his thoughts and feelings a mystery. My mother wasn't the same way. She wore her heart on her sleeve, let her tears cascade down her cheeks.

I approached them slowly, testing the waters to see if they wanted to speak to me right now.

My dad looked at me then opened his arm toward me, beckoning me to join their circle. He wrapped his arm around me and held my mother and me together. I was taller than my mother and the same height as my father, so we cushioned my mother in between us.

"Con..." My mom turned away from my father and moved into my chest instead. She hugged me tightly, her tears soaking into my t-shirt. "Thank you for getting her here so quickly."

"Of course." I ran my hand up and down her back. "You were a badass today, Mom. I've never seen anything like that."

"No one touches my babies and gets away with it," she said with a sniff. "Not my son...not my daughter."

My father only had eyes for her, watching her come apart against me. "Button, Vanessa will be alright."

"I know," my mother said. "But until I see her...I'll be a wreck."

MUSE WALKED INTO THE WAITING ROOM WITH Dante beside her. To everyone else, she looked exactly the same as before. But to me, she was glowing. Her flat stomach couldn't hide what was growing deep inside her.

What we made together.

My parents held each other through this ordeal, terrified their little girl wouldn't make it through the surgery.

Muse and I were just like them now. We made something together, and we would love something together.

She set her sights on me first, and like no one else was in the room, she ran up to me and landed against my chest, hitting me like a speeding car hits a brick wall. She clutched me, gripping my waist with strength I didn't realize she had.

My hand cupped the back of her head, and I pressed kisses to her hairline, showering her with plenty of affection right in front of my family. I didn't care if it made them uncomfortable. I didn't care if it was inappropriate.

"Have you heard anything?" she asked.

"No."

She sighed against my chest. "She's going to be okay, right?"

"Yes...I know she will." I tilted her head up to look at me, showing her the resolution in my eyes. "She's a tough-ass woman. She can hold her own. I know she'll get through it. She's way too proud to survive a kidnapping only to die on a surgical table."

"True."

I angled Muse's chin to meet my gaze so I could place a kiss on her mouth. Her affection filled me with joy, made me feel happy for a brief moment. I forgot all the shit going on around me and just concentrated on her kiss. The only reason I pulled away was because I forced myself to. I rubbed my nose against hers and stepped back.

My mom walked up to us, her eyes still puffy and red from crying on my father's shoulders. "Your father told me about the baby. I meant to call...but then all this stuff happened and—"

"Mom, don't worry about it," I said quickly. "We understand."

She wrapped her arm around Muse's shoulders and rested her head against hers. "I just want you to know how excited I am. Your baby will be beautiful and healthy, and I'm so happy to be a grandmother."

"Thank you," Muse whispered. "I can't even tell I'm pregnant, but I feel totally different."

"I felt the same way when Conway was growing inside me." She moved her arm around my waist too. "You guys are going to start your own family now. It's the time of your lives when you'll feel the most joy. I know from experience."

"Thanks, Mom," I said. "We might need a babysitter sometimes."

"And I would be delighted," she said. "Your father would too."

I chuckled. "He doesn't seem like a baby kinda guy."

"That's where you're wrong," she said. "When you were

born, all he wanted to do was play with you. He didn't care about work anymore. You were the most important thing in his life. It used to be me...but I was glad to make the transfer." She kissed me on the cheek. "And I know you'll be the same way. You have your father's hardness, his roughness." She placed her finger against my chest, right over my heart. "But you have his softness too."

18

VANESSA

I woke up to the sound of my monitor beeping.

It took me a few seconds to figure out where I was.

To remember how I got there.

Knuckles kidnapped me, and I made a run for it. I got shot during my escape, and my mother choked him to death right in front of my eyes. Conway carried me into the back seat of a taxi and got me to the hospital. By the time we arrived, I'd passed out.

I'd been in the dark the rest of the time.

Thick gauze was wrapped around my arm, covering my gunshot wound. A drip of morphine was running directly into my IV. I was in a private room with a window that was covered by the drapes.

My eyes landed on my father first, who was sitting still as a statue. His head rested back against the wall, and my mother slept across his lap. His beard was thick from not shaving, and despite his age and constant exposure to the sun, he resembled a young man—strong and in the throes of youth.

I watched him before he noticed me, remembering the way he stood up to Knuckles even with a gun pressed to his forehead. There was no way for him to know my mother was coming. He was simply brave—braver than all other men.

He came for me like I knew he would. And the only way he would have been in the area was if my clue had tipped him off. We worked together to get me out of there. Everyone had survived, except Knuckles.

I was glad he was dead.

And I was glad my mother spat on his face.

I would have done the same if I weren't so weak.

Conway and Sapphire were in the room too, Sapphire sitting on Conway's lap. He ran his fingers through her hair as she rested her head on his shoulder. Uncle Cane sat on the other couch with Aunt Adelina, their heads pressed close together.

I opened my mouth to speak, but my voice didn't come out. My mouth was just too dry. I tried again. "Dad…"

My father's eyes shifted to me at once, and the hardness on his face was instantly replaced by overwhelming joy. It was the same look he gave when he was proud of something I said or did. He shook my mother underneath him, his eyes staying on me. "Button, she's awake."

Mom jerked up immediately, her body waking up quicker than her brain did. "My baby…"

My father walked to me with his arm around my mom. He stood at my bedside and placed his hand against my chest, looking down at me with those same proud eyes. His hand was warm in comparison to the icy temperature of the room. "*Tesoro*…" It was a name he'd been calling me since I was little.

Sweetheart.

His thumb brushed across my hairline. "You're so strong…so strong like your mother." He leaned down and kissed me on the forehead. Then he wrapped his arms around me and hugged me, his chin resting on my head. "I'm so proud of you."

"Thanks, Dad," I said into his neck, smelling his cologne.

He kissed my forehead again. "Love you so much, *tesoro*."

"I love you too."

When my mom moved in next, the tears in her eyes were the size of raindrops. They splashed on my cheeks and rolled down my face. She held me close to her, crying quietly against me. "I'm so glad you're okay."

"Me too, Mama."

She smothered my forehead with kisses and continued to weep quietly.

My father rubbed her back, watching her embrace me.

My mom pulled away minutes later, her tears done but the aftereffects still present. With red and puffy eyes, she stepped back and sniffed.

"You're a badass, Mom," I said. "He was twice your size, and you dragged him across the ground."

"It's mama bear strength," she whispered. "Every woman has it when they think their little one is in trouble."

"But yes," my father said. "Your mother is a badass."

I chuckled then patted her arm. "Thanks for taking him out. I would have done it myself, but you beat me to the punch."

My brother came next, giving me a rare look of fondness he refused to show unless he had to. He grabbed my hand and smiled with his eyes. "You look really good. How's your arm?"

"It's alright," I said. "That morphine drip is doing wonders right now..."

"Yeah, I bet," he said with a chuckle. "You were really brave, Vanessa. Most women wouldn't have been so fearless."

"You're only fearless and brave when you have so much to lose. I wasn't going to let that weirdo keep me. And I wasn't going to let him have Sapphire either. Father taught me well. Knuckles shouldn't have underestimated me."

"No." Conway finally smiled. "You're right. He shouldn't have."

Sapphire came next, her waterworks going just like with my mother. "I'm so sorry about all this. It's all my fault and—"

"Hey, let it go," I said quickly. "I'm glad it happened. Now he's dead, and you never have to worry about him ever again. A lot of good came out of this. You're my family now, Sapphire. And families do everything for each other."

That seemed to make her tears well up, but for a whole new reason. "Thank you..."

"So I hear I'm getting a niece or nephew."

Sapphire rubbed her hand across her tummy, feeling a nonexistent bump. "Yeah...in about nine months we'll have another Barsetti."

"That's so great." I rested my hand on hers on her stomach. "You've already made my brother into a man, so I know you'll do right by his son or daughter. And I'll spoil the hell out of them. If it's a girl, I'll take her to the club and get her drunk for the first time. And if it's a boy, I'll take him to the shooting range."

Conway didn't like any of that and scowled. "I liked it better when you were unconscious."

"Funny. I liked it better when it was just Sapphire and me talking."

He rolled his eyes and stepped away. "She's already back to normal."

MY PARENTS WANTED ME TO RETURN TO TUSCANY with them for my recovery, but that just didn't seem feasible, especially since I wasn't supposed to fly anywhere. So I stayed with Conway and Sapphire outside of Verona.

It was a three-story villa, so it wasn't like they didn't have the room. I pretty much had the second floor all to myself. I spent my days in bed while Sapphire kept me company. She would sit at my bedside, and we would talk. When I was finally able to get out of bed, we would walk around the house or sit in the hot tub.

It would take a few weeks for my arm to heal, and doctors were more concerned about it getting infected than anything else.

My parents stayed in Milan, so they visited me all the time, along with my aunt and uncle.

People were making a much bigger deal than they needed to.

I was fine.

My arm hurt a little. No big deal.

But it was nice to spend so much time with my family.

We were having dinner together one night in the dining room, my parents visiting for the evening. Dante had made an Italian feast, just like he did every other night because he knew it was my favorite. Fresh baked bread, pasta with fresh truffles, and the best olive oil made in Italy.

Along with the best wine.

"Now that it's been a week, do you mind if I ask what happened?" Conway sat at the head of the table, Sapphire on his right side.

"No." My dad's deep voice ripped through the air like a sharpened knife. "She doesn't have to talk about it ever if she doesn't want to. Let's just enjoy our dinner."

I'd never told anyone the details because no one asked.

They were just relieved I was okay, and they were probably afraid to hear what I had to say. My face was swollen from the way Knuckles hit me so many times, but that wasn't too bad. But to a parent, that sounded like the end of the world. "I don't mind talking about it. There's not much to tell, honestly. I came home from school, and he was waiting for me. We exchanged a few words, and I casually went to the fridge because that's where my steak knife was hidden. When I shut the door, I stabbed him. I was aiming for his heart, but he turned quickly, and I missed. He knocked the knife out of my hand and then took me out of the apartment." I didn't share the part of the story where he hit me, knowing it would hurt my parents. "Then they transferred me to one place and then another...and I ended up at that apartment near the opera house. Knuckles told me he wanted to make the trade, and all I had to do was behave and I wouldn't get hurt. But you know me...I'm a bit of a shit talker." I chuckled and then ripped off another piece of bread. "I tried to get them to come into the bedroom with water more often, that way they would let me use the bathroom. But one of the henchmen insulted me, so I kicked him in the shin. When he faltered, I grabbed his gun and shot him in the head." I was craving a glass of red wine, but with my medication, I wasn't allowed to have any. I'd just admitted to everyone at the table that I killed someone, but I still didn't feel an ounce of contrition for what I'd done. If I hadn't killed him, he might have killed someone I loved. Or even me.

Everyone in my family wore blank expressions, unsure what to say in response to my tale.

My father took the lead. "You did the right thing, *tesoro*. Don't feel guilty about it."

"I don't, and I never will." My parents taught me to never show mercy. If I thought someone would ever grant me mercy, I would be disappointed.

"If you hadn't made a run for it, it would have taken us a lot longer to find you," Conway said. "And it could have gone down in a different way. We all made it out alive, with a few scratches and bruises."

"Mom told me never to wait for a man to rescue me. She said I always have to rely on myself to be free...and I listened to her." I held up my water glass, the only thing I was allowed to drink. "So this is for my mother. For being a badass."

Her eyes were filled with affection as she stared at me.

My father smiled and raised his glass. "I'll drink to that."

"Me too." Sapphire clinked her water glass against mine.

Conway followed suit and did the same thing. "For being a badass."

"Now you have to find a man that's badass enough for you," Sapphire said. "But I'm not sure if you'll find a man as good as the Barsettis."

"She probably won't," my father said. "But that's okay." He gave me a soft smile. "She's the kind of woman who doesn't need a man."

19

SAPPHIRE

VANESSA AND I SAT WITH OUR FEET IN THE HOT TUB. Neither of us could drink wine, so we settled for lemonade instead. Fall was in full effect now, so the warm sun had disappeared. Now there was a distinct chill in the air, and we wore sweaters and sweatpants that were rolled up to our knees.

"How's the arm?" I asked.

"Still stings but it's getting better," she said. "I have to sleep on my right side, and every time I turn over in the middle of the night, it hurts, so I have to roll back over... but it's not forever."

"Have you been sleeping well?"

"Minus the pain, great."

"That's good…any nightmares?"

"Nope." Vanessa wasn't putting up a façade for the world to see. She really was as strong as she projected, as powerful as she claimed to be. She was confident and centered, refusing to give in to fear or terror. "I'm just relieved he's gone. I never expected him to show up at my apartment, but now that he's dead, I never have to worry about him coming back."

"I'm glad he's dead too."

"With assholes like that, they should be buried in the ground. A part of me is glad all this happened. If he was going to stalk you for the rest of your life, that wouldn't have been right. Now you and Conway can raise your family without any concerns."

"I guess…but I wish it'd been me instead of you." I hated seeing the gauze wrapped around her arm. I hated knowing she couldn't drink wine because her medication was too strong. She was in the hospital for a few days because of me. She could have died because of me. Knuckles came into our lives because of me, and I hated seeing a Barsetti suffer because of it.

"I don't," she said seriously. "You're pregnant...that could have been bad."

"I know...but still."

"Girl, look at me." She snapped her fingers and directed two fingers at her eyes. "You're family now. And I would do anything to protect you and that little one inside. So don't feel guilty, okay?"

I smiled. "Well, my last name isn't Barsetti."

"Doesn't matter. And if it's never Barsetti, that doesn't matter either. You guys are a family. You're the mother of my niece or nephew. You're going to be part of our lives forever."

"You're so sweet. When I first met Conway, he wasn't that compassionate. He didn't have a gentle side to him at all. But the more I got to know him, the more I realized he's just trying to hide it as much as he can."

"You got that right. Conway pretends to be hard, but he's soft all the way through." She took another drink of her lemonade. "Ugh, I miss red wine. This is way too sweet. But water is too bland."

"What do you do when you aren't drinking wine?" I

asked with a chuckle. "You must drink water then, right?"

She shrugged. "No...wine is essential to my diet."

"Even in the morning?"

"If there's a leftover bottle from the night before...why not?"

I looked into the darkness and saw the landscape disappear. Out here, there wasn't another house within a few miles. The only thing that could be seen was the lights from Verona. But the rest of the world was just dark shapes and outlines. "Since you love wine so much, maybe you should think about joining your parents."

"I love to drink wine. Doesn't mean I love to make wine. And I want to explore other things before I settle on something easy. I know I would be happy making wine, but what if there's something else out there? Some experience I'm not enjoying because I didn't bother?"

"Good point. And you think painting could be your calling?"

"I'm not Picasso," she said. "But I'm decent. I just finished this piece of my parents working in the vineyards. It captures everything I love about Italy. I'll show it to you sometime. When you look at it, I don't think anyone would think it's a priceless piece of art. But it does tell a story...a great story. And there's gotta be someone out there who feels the same thing looking at it as I did painting it."

Vanessa wasn't just smart, but deep. She was confident, but she was also open to new things. She lived emotionally but logically at the same time. I hadn't seen her work, but judging by the way she spoke about it, it was her passion. "I'd love to see it."

"I'll bring it by next time. Did you know my namesake was an artist?"

"Your aunt?" I asked.

"Yes. My aunt Vanessa was a painter. She'd make these images, but she would incorporate buttons into her pieces. My father still has them up in his study. I wouldn't call them masterpieces, but they're beautiful."

"Is that what inspired you to paint?"

She looked off into the distance as she considered it for a long time. She took another drink of her lemonade then licked her lips. "I guess it did. I used to see those paintings as a little girl. Maybe that did have something to do with it."

"I'm sorry your family has been through so much tragedy. It's another reason why I feel terrible dragging you into it."

"You shouldn't beat yourself up over it. My parents want men like Knuckles to be dead anyway. Now that he's gone, the world is a little prettier. If you weren't his victim, someone else would be, right?"

"Yeah."

"So, the world has given us so much, and now we've given something back."

I chuckled. "Good way to look at it."

"So, are you going to be in the fashion show on Saturday?"

"Conway and I haven't talked about it, actually. With everything going on...it just slipped my mind."

"You should do it."

"You think?" I asked. "I'm not sure if my mind is playing tricks on me, but I feel like I'm starting to show a little..."

"I think you are too. But that's a good thing. It's sexy."

"That's what Conway says..."

"And he's right. This is one of the only times I'm going to agree with him. Pregnant women are so beautiful. Whether they're modeling lingerie or umbrellas, that baby bump is hot."

"Well, thanks. That gives me a boost of confidence."

Conway stepped out the back door and walked toward us, wearing his black sweatpants with a matching t-shirt. He stopped at the end of the tub with his hands in his pockets. "Enjoying your evening?"

"I was telling your woman she needs to be in the show on Saturday," Vanessa said. "She thinks her little belly will be a turn-off, but I don't agree."

Conway looked down at his sister, a slight smile on his face. "I can't believe I'm going to say this, but I actually agree with her. And if you're wondering, that never happens."

"Because I'm extremely intelligent, and he's a little dull," Vanessa said. "So we just don't see eye to eye."

The playfulness in his eyes turned into a small glare. "I love having you around all the time…"

Vanessa grinned. "I know you do, brother."

"So what are you going to do about the show?" I asked. "It's only a few days away. Did you postpone it?"

"No, I couldn't postpone it," he answered. "I have an alternate in place if you aren't up for it. So it's your call."

"Mine?" I asked in surprise.

"Yeah." He stood tall, his chiseled arms contrasting against the dark color of his shirt. "I know you have the dance moves down. Just a few more practice runs, and you should be fine. But again, it's up to you."

"Well, what do you want me to do, Conway?"

He shrugged. "I'd like you to be in the show, but if you'd rather not, that's okay too."

I wanted to skip the spotlight. I preferred to stay home and enjoy the peacefulness of the house. All I cared about was the baby growing inside me. I wanted to start preparing for the baby's room, getting all the supplies for when the baby arrived. But making one final appearance would be great for Conway's career. After everything he did for me, it was the least I could do. "I want to do it."

I STOOD IN FRONT OF THE MIRROR IN MY PANTIES, checking my stomach from different angles. If anyone else looked at me, they wouldn't notice the difference in my figure. I was still thin with a fairly flat stomach. But when I glided my hands down, I could feel the slight rise. It was hardly noticeable, but it was there.

Conway emerged behind me, his figure visible in the mirror. "What are you doing?"

"Trying to see if I'm showing."

He stopped behind me and placed his hand over my stomach. His hands were twice as big as mine and easily covered my entire tummy. His fingertips were rough from poking himself with needles for the last decade. "I can tell."

"You can?"

"Not by much. Just a little."

"Do you think people will notice at the show?" I placed my hand over his.

"I hope they do." He rested his chin on my head and looked at my stomach in the mirror. His fingers gently brushed across the skin, feeling the little bump that no one else could distinguish. "Do you think it's a boy or a girl?"

"No idea."

"They say mothers just know."

"Well, I don't know the baby well enough to take a guess."

"You will soon enough."

"What do you think it is?" I asked.

"Not sure. My family line has produced more boys than girls, so maybe a boy."

"Mine is about even. Do you want a son?"

"Yes," he admitted. "I do want a son. But I want a daughter too."

My eyes shifted up to his face, feeling the sweet surprise erupt in my veins. "You want another one...?"

His eyes met mine in the mirror. "Yes. Can't just have one, right?"

"I just...I figured that conversation would happen much later."

"Well, Carter and I are nearly identical in age, so it's made us really close. Vanessa and I are seven years apart. She and I have a good relationship, but if we were closer to the same age, we would have experienced more together. So, I always thought if I had one child, I would immediately have another."

"So, you want to have another baby right away?" I asked, my eyebrow rising.

"Yeah, I guess so."

I had been terrified to tell him I was pregnant in the first place, and now he was talking about having another baby. Perhaps that time apart was the best thing for us. He had wanted to avoid sharing his life with someone, keeping his commitment to his bachelor life and his work. But now that he couldn't live without me, his priorities changed. "I wouldn't mind that." It would be a lot of sleepless nights, but I was still happy to start my own family. I didn't have anyone once my brother died, and now I could start over.

"Good." He walked to the bed and set his alarm on his phone. His sweatpants and boxers came off before he got into bed. He'd been back at the office for the last week while I stayed home with Vanessa. His show was this Saturday, so he couldn't afford to stop. He lay in bed then folded his hands under his head.

I got into bed beside him, feeling at peace now that everything was over. No one was chasing me anymore. Vanessa was safe. Conway wasn't pissed at me because I was pregnant. His family was happy about it. Everything was going well.

He studied my face, his handsome expression soft.

"What?" I whispered.

"I'm just looking at you."

"You look at me a lot."

"And you look at me a lot," he countered.

"Well, there's a lot to look at..." My hand touched his chest, feeling the hard muscle underneath the warm skin. I'd never seen a man so beautiful. Nox was a handsome man, but he didn't get my heart beating the way Conway did. No one did.

"I'm glad my sister is staying with us and getting better, but I look forward to the day she leaves."

"You don't mean that."

"I do. She's hogging you."

"I like spending time with her. She's my friend, not just your sister."

He released a sigh under his breath. "I don't like you having friends."

"You want me to be lonely forever?"

"No. You have me." His hand moved to my stomach. "You have a family."

"Are you going to be jealous too when I spend more time with the baby than you?"

"As long as I'm there too, no." His hand moved down and played with the strings of my panties. He felt the lace in his fingertips before he pulled it over my hip. He gripped the material with his large hand and then tugged it over my ass and then down my legs. He moved closer to me on the bed, moaning quietly before he even had me. He must have felt the wetness in my panties with his fingertips, the sign that I'd wanted him for the last thirty minutes.

He moved on top of me and welcomed himself between my legs. His long cock pressed against my wet folds, moving through them slowly. When he held his heavy physique on top of me, his biceps tightened and the other muscles flexed and popped with veins. He tilted his hips and pressed the crown of his cock inside me, meeting the moisture that already started to pool for him. Then he slid inside, inching all the way until every bit was buried inside me.

My ankles locked together behind his back, and I stared at the greedy look in his eyes. My nipples were hard with arousal, and my pussy tightened at his large intrusion. Sometimes I knew I was going to come before we even started.

He started to thrust, moving gentle and slow. "Tell me you love me."

My tits shook with his movements, and I felt his cock pierce me deep inside before it pulled out again. When I'd confessed my deepest feelings, it ripped us apart. But now he got off on it, got off on my affection. "I love you..."

"Tell me you'll always love me."

"Always," I whispered.

"Tell me I'm the only man you'll ever have."

My hands locked around his neck, and I moved with him. "Only you."

I DIDN'T FEEL SELF-CONSCIOUS IN THE LINGERIE because I was used to being photographed in it. My pregnancy was hardly noticeable, so I didn't think anyone would see that. None of the other girls said anything, but then again, they still hated me so they wouldn't mention anything even if I were nine months pregnant.

They seemed to hate me even more than they did before, probably because they thought I was going to be gone for good when I left for those three months. Having me back was a slap in the face all over again.

We went through the show from beginning to end a few times, doing it with the lights, music, and smoke machines. I'd only done one show before, so I was nervous about doing this one. I could just tell Conway I didn't want to do it, but since Lacey betrayed him, I had to make her pay for her decision. I needed Conway to be successful because it was so important to him. Having me on that stage would get people talking—and that's what he needed.

These heels killed my feet, but whatever. I could pull through.

At the end of rehearsals, I yanked the shoes off and let my feet flatten again.

If my feet could cry, there would be tears all over the floor.

Conway appeared at the stairs to the stage, dressed in a navy blue suit and looking handsome like always. His hands rested in his pockets. "You look perfect up there. I think this show will be the best one yet."

"I'm sure it will be." I massaged the bottom of my feet then gave them a break. The pair of heels were placed beside me. I was dressed in a black corset with a diamond necklace. It killed my waistline, but it was less torturous than standing on my feet.

"You alright?"

"Yeah, my feet just need a break."

He eyed me before he bent down and scooped me up into his arms.

"What are you doing?"

"You needed a lift." He grabbed the shoes then carried me up the stairs and to the backstage area. He moved past the girls as they undressed, hiding their usual glares since Conway was there.

I never complained about the way the girls treated me because I didn't feel the need to stoop to their level. Conway was already mine. It wasn't like I felt threatened by them.

He set me down at my changing station and placed my heels on the counter.

"One more day of rehearsals and it'll be over."

"No rehearsals tomorrow."

"Really? Why not?"

"Tomorrow is a day of rest. The girls don't eat, and they cleanse their bodies to look as skinny as possible."

I cocked an eyebrow. "You expect me to do that?"

The only reaction he gave was a smile. "No."

"Good. Because that wasn't going to happen. I wonder what we should do with our day off."

"I have something in mind."

"What?"

"You want to take a ride to that hilltop and see Verona?" he asked. "Dante can pack us a lunch. The weather is supposed to be nice tomorrow. Not warm like in the summer, but sunny enough."

There was nothing I wanted to do more. I knew my days of activity were coming to an end. My belly would get big, and I'd sit around more as I waited for the baby to come. I wanted to enjoy being outdoors as much as possible. "Yes, I'd love that."

He smiled. "I thought you would. We'll have Carbine take us there."

I WORE THE SAME JEANS I WORE TO THE STABLES because they were thick and warm. They were perfect for working outside, so they were perfect for riding on the back of a horse. I wore a thick, long-sleeved shirt and a sweater for extra warmth. I hadn't worn my boots in ages, so I pulled those on too.

I walked downstairs and noticed the smells in the kitchen. Pots and pans were simmering on the stove, and the oven contained something else. It seemed like Dante was preparing an entire feast rather than a picnic. "Wow, what are you making?"

Dante held up the picnic basket. "I've got a lot of great things for you two on your ride for today."

I glanced at all the burners and the oven. "Looks like you're making Christmas dinner."

He smiled and then held up a loaf of fresh bread. "Special bread. Takes forever to make, but it's delicious." He dodged the question and didn't seem like he was ever going to answer it. "Did you need something, Sapphire?"

"I was going to ask if you could pack some wine for Conway. He won't drink around me, but I'd like him to enjoy something."

"Of course, Sapphire. I'll think of something nice."

"Thanks." I walked back into the hallway and ran into Vanessa. "Hey, how are you feeling today?"

"Really good." Her hair was done, and her makeup was heavier than usual. She wore a black dress with a gold bracelet. The only thing missing were heels. She was barefoot. "It's the first day when I haven't needed to pop some painkillers. Those pills are so big and difficult to swallow."

"I'm glad you're feeling better."

"Me too. I know Conway wants me out of your hair as soon as possible."

"Not true."

She laughed. "Yes, it is. And that's okay. He told me off for hogging you last night."

I rolled my eyes. "Ignore him. He's a weirdo."

She laughed again. "I'm glad you finally realize it. So, you guys are going on a ride?"

"Yeah. There's this nice spot in the hills where we can see a great view of Verona."

"That's nice. You guys have fun." She started to walk down the hallway. "I won't keep you."

"Vanessa?"

"Yeah?" She turned back around.

"Are you going somewhere? You look so nice."

"Oh." She looked down at herself then smoothed out her dress. "I've been in my sweats for so long that I just wanted to look nice for a change. I'm feeling really good, you know?"

"Well, it definitely shows." I went upstairs to meet Conway, and then together, we walked down to the stables with the picnic basket Dante packed for us. The air was cold but not unbearable. When the sun was right on us, it became the perfect temperature.

"When I went into the kitchen, it looked like Dante was making a feast. I hope all that work wasn't for this lunch."

Conway saddled Carbine and placed all our stuff in the pack. In tight jeans, boots, and a long-sleeved black shirt, he looked like a perfect fit out in the stables. He wore a suit better than anyone else, but he could dress down and look just as sexy casual. "He's probably preparing dinner."

"But it's just the three of us."

He shrugged. "Dante takes his chef responsibilities very

seriously. Sometimes he makes a simple dinner, and at other times, he likes to make a gourmet feast. Maybe it's because Vanessa is feeling better. Wants to celebrate."

"That's true."

We took Carbine to the trail and then we both mounted the horse. I sat behind Conway, my arms wrapped around his waist. It didn't rain yesterday, so the soil was fairly dry. We took our time down the trail, slowly moving up into the small hills so we could find the perfect spot.

I rested my cheek against his neck and kept my arms secured around his hard waist. I felt his back rise and fall every time he breathed. His cologne was potent, and once it was mixed with sweat, it reminded me of sex. "It's so beautiful up here."

"You never get tired of it."

We rode for an hour before we reached the hilltop. Right underneath the oak was a spot of soft grass. We let Carbine graze while Conway unpacked the blanket and the picnic lunch.

It was a clear day after several days of storms, and the view of the city was crisp. The rooftops shone under the light just the way they did in summer. We were too far away to see the details, like people walking to the shops. But we could see the cars reflect the light of the sun as they moved around. "Beautiful."

Conway set up the picnic on the blanket, and together, we enjoyed the sandwiches and salads Dante prepared for us. Conway pulled out a bottle of apple cider and poured two glasses.

"I asked Dante to pack you some wine."

"I know," he said with a smile. "And I told him to take it back."

"Con, you can drink around me."

"No. I really don't mind." He drank his juice without complaint. "There's plenty of times when I sneak off and have a date with my scotch, so don't feel too bad for me."

"So there is another woman in your life?"

He smiled. "I guess so."

I finished my sandwich then moved on to my salad. I ate more than I should, especially as there was going to be a show tomorrow, but since I was pregnant, I didn't care.

Any extra weight I put on could be attributed to the baby.

Or, at least, that was how I could spin it.

We finished lunch, and Conway packed everything up and placed the basket off to the side. Then we sat close together, his arm around my shoulder. Together, we stared at the city, my head resting on his shoulder.

"Nine months ago, my life was so different." He stared at the scene in front of us, reliving a distant memory. "Selfish and living a life of solitude, my existence was really simple. All I cared about was success and money. But I can honestly say I was happy. I'd become the man I always wanted to be. I didn't need to rely on my parents to start my own business. I did everything on my own—and my family was proud."

I didn't understand where this was going, but I didn't interrupt him because I wanted to find out. Conway was a man of few words. He conveyed his thoughts with his expressions most of the time. Right now, his gaze was unreadable.

"But then I set my sights on you...and everything changed. Even when I saw you standing on that stage, my life shifted. You became my focal point, my muse.

And after that, everything went into free fall. My simple and predictable life was no longer what it used to be. I made exceptions and changes to accommodate you. I fought my attraction to you, worked so hard to hold on to my old life. And then I paid a fortune for you, and I knew in my heart I wouldn't have done that for anyone else. I could even say that was the moment I knew...the moment I knew there was no going back."

My hand moved to his thigh, and I gripped the muscle through his jeans.

"I don't know when I fell in love with you. I just know it happened a long time ago, and I kept lying to myself to avoid the truth. I know I loved you when we were in Greece. I know I loved you when I watched you work in the stables from my window. I know I loved you when you asked me to make love to you and I listened."

"Conway..." I closed my eyes, touched by his sweetness.

"And I know I'm going to love you for the rest of my life." He moved his hand into his left pocket and pulled out a small box.

Oh my god.

Anytime a man pulled out a small box, it only meant

one thing.

This was really happening.

"Conway..."

He opened the box and revealed a diamond ring. It was enormous, the biggest rock I'd ever seen in person. At least two karats of a single flawless diamond, along with smaller diamonds along the band. Made of white gold and sparkly, it was gorgeous. It was so gorgeous I wasn't even sure what to do. "Muse, I would ask you to marry me, but I'm not going to give you the opportunity to say no. So I'm telling you to marry me." He grabbed my left hand and slipped the ring onto my finger. "You will be Mrs. Barsetti. You will be my wife. And you will be mine."

I felt the weight instantly. I'd never worn jewelry, and now I was carrying something heavy and meaningful. I pulled the ring closer to me, examining the way it felt on my finger. Beautiful and perfect, it was something I didn't even know I wanted. I didn't care for flashy or expensive things, but Conway wanted the world to know I was his wife by the way he decorated me. "I don't know what to say..." I didn't realize I was crying until a large tear splashed onto my hand.

"Don't say anything." He clasped his hand in mine. "Just be mine. The way you've always been mine."

We returned to the house and handed Carbine over to Marco.

All I could think about was the ring on my finger. It was a piece of jewelry, but it symbolized so much. Listening to Conway demand I marry him rather than ask was even better. Why ask when he knew what my answer would be.

He hooked his arm around my waist and walked with me back to the house, his face close to mine. "I thought we would have a romantic dinner."

"Dinner?" I asked. "I don't want dinner." I stopped walking and circled my arms around his neck. "I want to go to bed with you. I want to make love with your ring sitting on my finger. Dante can leave dinner outside the door. Maybe we'll get to it...but I suspect we won't."

He stopped walking and pivoted his body toward mine. He circled his arms around my waist, gave me a soft smile, and then pressed his forehead to mine. "As tempting as that sounds, we have other plans."

"We do?"

"Yeah." He kissed my hairline and pulled me inside the house. When we walked into the dining room, his entire family was there. The table was decorated with beautiful vases of flowers, and there was a sign pinned to the wall that read, "Congratulations." They all threw their hands in the air and shouted with excitement. Conway's parents were there, grinning with touched expressions in their eyes. Vanessa held up a half-drunk bottle of wine and yelled at the top of her lungs. Carter and Carmen clapped, and his aunt and uncle looked just as happy.

"What a surprise..." I clutched my chest, seeing all these amazing people gathered around for us. "Your family is so wonderful."

Conway looked down at me, his eyes narrowing in fondness. He pressed his forehead to mine and whispered so only I could hear. "Now they're your family too."

THE BARSETTIS KNEW HOW TO DRINK WINE AND celebrate. The fun didn't die down until after midnight, so Conway and I didn't get into bed until one in the morning. Now that this ring was on my finger, I had no intention of taking it off. I dropped my clothes on the ground and got into bed.

Conway did the same, stripping down until he was just in his skin. He got into bed beside me, and despite how late it was, he was hard like sex was still on his mind. He dragged me to the center of the bed before he spread my thighs with his knees. "The ring looks good on you."

"It feels good too."

"I was thinking we could get married soon. Something small on the terrace."

I hadn't been engaged for a day, so I hadn't thought about the wedding. But it didn't make sense to wait, not when I had so few people in my life. It would just be his family and a few friends. "The sooner, the better. I don't want to look like a cow in my wedding dress."

He glared at me.

"You know what I mean."

"That's not why I want to get married soon. I just want to be married."

My hands ran up his chest, and I locked my ankles together around his back. "Me too."

"I want you to wear your ring tomorrow. I'm going to announce our engagement and the baby."

After the festivities of the day, the show hadn't even crossed my mind. "Is that why you asked me today?"

The corner of his mouth rose in a smile. "Yes. I want to tell the world you're mine. What would be a better time to do that?"

"Sounds possessive to me."

"So what if it is?" he challenged. His eyes darkened in a sexy way, brooding and powerful.

Conway had always been possessive of me, but now it was at a more intense level. I loved this man with all my heart, and it felt wonderful knowing he felt the same way. He wasn't afraid to tell me how much he loved me, to wear his heart on his sleeve. He was the only man I'd ever been with, and I was the only woman he'd ever loved. "That's fine with me."

20

VANESSA

AFTER THE SHOW ENDED, CONWAY AND SAPPHIRE spent most of their time in their bedroom.

Getting nasty.

I felt like I was encroaching on this special time, so I decided to pack my bags and return to my apartment in Milan. It had been nice recovering in my brother's beautiful home, and Dante did an excellent job taking care of me, but I was feeling a lot better.

It was time to return to class and catch up on everything I missed before we got to winter break.

My arm was pretty much back to normal. It was a little

shaky when I moved it, but I needed to get it back to its previous strength if I wanted to keep painting. I wasn't on the painkillers anymore, and now the gauze was gone from my arm. All that was left was a nasty scar.

I placed all my things by the door then broke the news to my brother and future sister-in-law over lunch. "I'm heading back home. I'm back on my feet and ready to return to class. I appreciate everything you guys have done for me."

"You're leaving?" Sapphire asked incredulously. "But you've only been here for a few weeks. You can't go."

"Look, I'm fine." I sat across from them at the table, my salad only half eaten. "Really. You guys should enjoy this time together anyway. When's the wedding?"

"Don't change the subject," Sapphire said. "You should stay with us until you're a hundred percent."

"I am," I said. "I need to catch up on the time I missed from class. I haven't been to my apartment in forever... there's stuff I need to do."

"You're really going to stay there?" my brother asked in surprise. "After what happened?"

"I'm not letting some dead psychopath chase me out of my home," I said. "It's a great apartment. It's walking distance from everything, and it's a nice neighborhood. Besides, I hate moving anyway."

"Are you sure?" Conway asked. "Because—"

"I'm fine," I said. "I'm not just trying to be a tough cookie."

Conway finally stopped pressing me.

"Besides, this is a special time for you guys," I said. "I want you to enjoy each other without worrying about me."

"But we love having you here," Sapphire said. "Honestly."

Conway shrugged.

"Ignore him," Sapphire said. "He loves you."

I smiled at my brother. "I know he does, even though he rarely shows it."

"Is there anything we can do to change your mind?" Sapphire asked, her eyes full of sincerity.

I shook my head. "No. But if I need anything, I'll let you know."

They finally dropped the argument, letting me have my freedom.

"When are you leaving?" Conway asked.

"After lunch." I was eager to get home and fix up the place. There was still a bloody knife somewhere.

"Have you thought about going to therapy?" My brother sipped his water, refusing to drink alcohol around Sapphire since she couldn't have any.

I rolled my eyes. "I don't need therapy."

"There's no shame in it," Sapphire said. "You've been through a lot."

"I don't think less of people who go to therapy, but I really don't need it." My father taught me to be strong, and I wasn't letting some asshole make me feel unsafe. I got away when he kidnapped me, and there was no one in the world who had power over me. "Don't worry about me. If I need help, I'll ask."

"No, you won't," Conway jabbed. "You never ask for help."

I smiled because I knew he was right. I was far too stubborn, far too proud. But I liked being that way. "You're right. But I promise you, I'll be alright."

THE DRIVE BACK TO MILAN FELT LONGER THAN IT normally did, probably because I hadn't made the journey in so long. But it felt nice to be behind the wheel, to watch the countryside pass. It was overcast and chilly, but the weather couldn't diminish the natural beauty of Italy.

My arm hurt a bit when I turned the wheel, but it wasn't enough to make me think twice about it.

I spent most of my time thinking about my brother and Sapphire.

And how in love they were.

I knew Sapphire loved my brother for the man underneath the suit. She didn't care about his money or his success. She put up with his bad attitude and bullshit and saw the goodness underneath. Andrew Lexington had offered her a great living in America, and she could have just stayed there.

But she wanted to be with Conway.

I wouldn't lie to myself and say I wasn't jealous. I was very young and still had nearly a decade to settle down and find Mr. Right. I was very picky, so it was important to take my time. Looks were important, but they weren't everything. I was looking for a man similar to the men in my family—hard men who were strong and proud...with a bit of a heart underneath. That sounded so simple, but in reality, it was actually very hard to find.

Very.

And even if I did find a man I actually loved, getting my father's approval would be another obstacle.

He was pickier than I was.

But nonetheless, I wanted to fall in love, get married, and start a family of my own.

It would happen someday. Beautiful things like that couldn't be rushed.

My thoughts entertained me for the whole drive, and I pulled into the parking spot in my apartment complex. I almost never used my car, but my father insisted I have one. I grabbed my bags and stepped inside my apartment.

It was exactly as I left it.

The bloody knife was still on the kitchen floor, and I could even see the imprint of Knuckles's body in the couch from where he sat. My apartment smelled differently, like his scent still lingered in the place.

I washed off the knife and returned it to the fridge—just in case I needed it again. Then I cracked the window to get some air in the apartment. It was way too stuffy, and it missed my feminine touch. I needed to go to the market and put out a few vases of flowers.

I stood at the counter and looked around, feeling alone now that I was home. I enjoyed my solitude and independence. I loved exploring the city on my own. I loved my friends and experiencing the unknown.

But anytime I left my family, it was like a piece of me was left behind.

I needed some time on my own, time to find out who I really was. But once my soul-searching was over, I knew there was only one place I wanted to be.

In Tuscany with my parents.

I pictured living there with my husband and kids, right down the road so we could all be together. The man I fell in love with would have to be okay with that, and if he really loved me, he would do that for me.

Even if I met him here—in Milan.

The story continues in Empress in Lingerie...

I'm Vanessa Barsetti, the daughter of the infamous Crow Barsetti.

My father taught me how to fight. If a man lays a hand on me, I'll put him in his grave. As a Barsetti, I'm proud, stubborn, and don't take nonsense from anybody.

I walk home from a bar and take the wrong path.

And witness a brutal crime.

The murderer won't let me go. He's handsome, lethal, and

terrifying. With tattoos on his forearms and a presence full of threat, he's a shade of evil I've never encountered. And then he tells me the most terrifying thing of all.

His name is Bones.

Printed in Great Britain
by Amazon

44749631R00199